"The author delivers the goods: ... ...on scenes, dialogue that breathes, characters with heart and characters who eat those hearts, and glints of unforgiving humor. . . . Ed McBain owns this turf."

—***New York Times Book Review***

"Amazing. . . . McBain's telegraphic style gives his story a hard, reportorial surface. Characters are caught in a few memorable strokes; things happen economically. What is surprising in such terse circumstances is how much you have felt, or have been led to understand that the characters were feeling."

—***Los Angeles Times***

"Familiarity with the cops of the 87th Precinct builds something like devotion: the more we know about them the more we want to know." —***Newsweek***

"It is hard to think of anyone better at what he does. In fact, it's impossible." —**Robert B. Parker**

"The McBain stamp: sharp dialogue and crisp plotting."

—***Miami Herald***

"No one writes dialogue among cops as convincingly as McBain." —***Chicago Sun-Times***

"A ... ***...nes***

. . .

"McBain is a skillful writer who excels at pace, plot, and, especially, the complex clockwork of a cop's mind."

—***People***

"I never read Ed McBain without the awful thought that I still have a lot to learn. And when you think you're catching up, he gets better."

—Tony Hillerman

"McBain has a great approach, great attitude, terrific style, strong plots, excellent dialogue, sense of place, and sense of reality."

—Elmore Leonard

"Nobody writes better detective fiction than Ed McBain. Nobody."

—***West Coast Review of Books***

"McBain's characters age, change, and stay interesting."

—***Arizona Daily Star***

"McBain is the unquestioned king. . . . Light-years ahead of anyone else in the field."

—***San Diego Union-Tribune***

"No living mystery writer creates more suspenseful scenes or builds plots better than McBain."

—***Greensboro News & Record***

"McBain is a pro, at the top of his game."

—***Los Angeles Daily News***

"You'll be engrossed by McBain's fast, lean prose."

—***Chicago Tribune***

"Ed McBain is a national treasure."

—***Mystery News***

"McBain redefines the American police novel. . . . He can stop you dead in your tracks with a line of dialogue."

—***Cleveland Plain Dealer***

"McBain has stood the test of time. He remains one of the very best."

—***San Antonio Express-News***

"The hot-wire style has kept McBain ahead of the competition for three decades."

—***Philadelphia Inquirer***

"He keeps getting better. . . . His plots have become more complicated, and he juggles his subplots, his sidebar stories, with practiced—and improved—skill and surety. . . . McBain remains a literary boss on his chosen turf."

—***Tulsa World***

"McBain has . . . an unfailing ability to create tricky, engaging plots."

—***Roanoke Times & World-News***

ED McBAIN

Let's Hear It for the Deaf Man

WARNER BOOKS

The city in these pages is imaginary. The people, the places are all fictitious. Only the police routine is based on established investigatory technique.

WARNER BOOKS EDITION

Cover art and design by Tony Greco

Permission to use the photo on pages 24 and 38 has been granted by United States Press International; the photo on pages 88 and 112 by the Imperial War Museum, London; the photo on pages 129 and 166 by the Museum of Modern Art Film Stills Archive; and the photo on page 200 by Otto Hagel at *Life* magazine, © Time, Inc.

Warner Books, Inc.
1271 Avenue of the Americas
New York, NY 10020

Visit our Web site at
www.twbookmark.com

A Time Warner Company

Printed in the United States of America

First Paperback Printing: January 2001

10 9 8 7 6 5 4 3 2 1

This is for Murray Weller

Let's Hear It for the Deaf Man

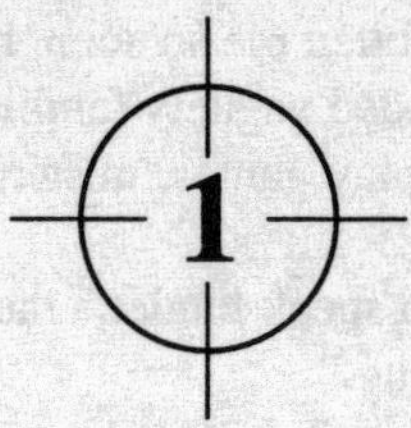

Fat balmy breezes wafted in off the park across the street, puffing lazily through the wide-open windows of the squadroom. It was the fifteenth of April, and the temperature outside hovered in the mid-sixties. Sunshine splashes drenched the room. Meyer Meyer sat at his desk idly reading a D.D. report, his bald pate touched with golden light, a beatific smile on his mouth, even though he was reading about a mugging. Cheek cradled on the heel and palm of his hand, elbow bent, blue eyes scanning the typewritten form, he sat in sunshine like a Jewish angel on the roof of the *Duomo*. When the telephone rang, it sounded like the trilling of a thousand larks, such was his mood this bright spring day.

"Detective Meyer," he said, "87th Squad."

"I'm back," the voice said.

"Glad to hear it," Meyer answered. "Who is this?"

"Come, come, Detective Meyer," the voice said. "You haven't forgotten me so soon, have you?"

The voice sounded vaguely familiar. Meyer frowned. "I'm too busy to play games, mister," he said. "Who is this?"

"You'll have to speak louder," the voice said. "I'm a little hard of hearing."

Nothing changed. Telephones and typewriters, filing cabinets, detention cage, water cooler, wanted posters, fingerprint equipment, desks, chairs, all were still awash in brilliant sunshine. But despite the floating golden motes, the room seemed suddenly bleak, as though that remembered telephone voice had stripped the place of its protective gilt to expose it as shabby and cheap. Meyer's frown deepened into a scowl. The telephone was silent except for a small electrical crackling. He was alone in the squadroom and could not initiate a trace. Besides, past experience had taught him that this man (if indeed he was who Meyer thought he was) would not stay on the line long enough for fancy telephone company acrobatics. He was beginning to wish he had not answered the telephone, an odd desire for a cop on duty. The silence lengthened. He did not know quite what to say. He felt foolish and clumsy. He could think only, My *God*, it's happening again.

"Listen," he said, "who is this?"

"You *know* who this is."

"No, I do not."

"In that case, you're even more stupid than I surmised." There was another long silence.

"Okay," Meyer said.

"Ahh," the voice said.

"What do you want?"

"Patience, patience," the voice said.

"Damn it, what do you *want?*"

"If you're going to use profanity," the voice said, "I won't talk to you at all."

There was a small click on the line.

Meyer looked at the dead phone in his hand, sighed, and hung up.

If you happen to be a cop, there are some people you don't need.

The Deaf Man was one of those people. They had not needed him the first time he'd put in an appearance, wreaking havoc across half the city in an aborted attempt to rob a bank. They had not needed him the next time, either, when he had killed the Parks Commissioner, the Deputy Mayor, and a handful of others in an elaborate extortion scheme that had miraculously backfired. They did not need him now; *whatever* the hell he was up to, they definitely did not need him.

"Who needs him?" Detective-Lieutenant Peter Byrnes asked. "Right now, I don't need him. Are you sure it was him?"

"It sounded like him."

"I don't need him when I got a cat burglar," Byrnes said. He rose from his desk and walked to the open windows. In the park across the street lovers were idly strolling, young mothers were pushing baby buggies, little girls were skipping rope, and a patrolman chatted with a man walking his dog. "I don't need him," Byrnes said again, and sighed. He turned from the window abruptly. He was a compact man, with hair more white than gray, broad-shouldered, squat, with rough-hewn features and flinty blue eyes. He gave an impression of controlled power, as though a violence within had been tempered, honed, and later protectively sheathed. He grinned suddenly, surprising Meyer. "If he calls again," Byrnes said, "tell him we're out."

"Very funny," Meyer said.

"Anyway, we don't even know it's him yet."

"I think it was him," Meyer said.

"Well, let's see if he calls again."

"If it's him," Meyer said with certainty, "he'll call again."

"Meanwhile, what about this goddamn burglar?" Byrnes said. "He's going to walk off with every building on Richardson if we don't get him soon."

"Kling's over there now," Meyer said.

"As soon as he gets back, I want a report," Byrnes said.

"What do I do about the Deaf Man?"

Byrnes shrugged. "Listen to him, find out what he wants." He grinned again, surprising Meyer yet another time. "Maybe he wants to turn himself in."

"Yeah," Meyer said.

Richardson Drive was a side street behind Silvermine Oval. There were sixteen large apartment buildings on that street, and a dozen of them had been visited by the cat burglar during the past two months.

According to police mythology, burglars are the cream of the criminal crop. Skilled professionals, they are capable of breaking and entering in a wink and without a whisper, making on-the-spot appraisals of appliances or jewelry, ripping off an entire apartment with speed and dexterity, and then vanishing soundlessly into the night. According to further lore, they are gentlemen one and all, rarely moved to violence unless cornered or otherwise provoked. To hear the police talk about burglars (except junkie burglars, who are usually desperate amateurs), one would guess that the job required rigorous training, intense dedication, enormous self-discipline, and extraordinary courage. (Not for nothing had the phrase "the guts of a burglar" entered everyday language directly from police lexicon.) This grudging respect, this tip of the investigatory hat, was completely in evidence that afternoon of April 15, when Detective Bert Kling talked to Mr. and Mrs. Joseph Angieri in their apartment at 638 Richardson Drive.

"Clean as a whistle," he said, and raised his eyebrows in admiration. He was referring to the fact that there were no chisel marks on any of the windows, no lock cylinders punched out, no evidence of any fancy glass cutter or crowbar work. "Did you lock all the doors and windows when you went away?" he asked.

"Yes," Angieri said. He was a man in his late fifties, wearing a wildly patterned short-sleeved shirt, and sporting a deep suntan, both of which he had acquired in Jamaica. "We always lock up," he said. "This is the city."

Kling looked at the door lock again. It was impossible to force this type of lock with a celluloid strip, nor were there any pick marks on it. "Anybody else have a key to this apartment?" he asked, closing the door.

"Yes. The super. He's got a key to every apartment in the building."

"I meant besides him," Kling said.

"My mother has a key," Mrs. Angieri said. She was a short woman, slightly younger than her husband, her eyes darting anxiously in her tanned face. She was,

Kling knew, reacting to the knowledge that she had been burglarized—that someone had violated this private space, someone had entered her home and roamed it with immunity, had handled her possessions, had taken things rightfully belonging to her. The *loss* was not the important factor; the jewelry was probably covered by insurance. It was the *idea* that staggered her. If someone could enter to steal, what would prevent someone from entering to kill?

"Might she have been here while you were away? Your mother?"

"What for?"

"I don't know. Just to look in . . ."

"No."

"Water the plants . . ."

"We don't keep plants," Angieri said.

"Besides, my mother's eighty-four years old," Mrs. Angieri said. "She hardly ever leaves Riverhead. That's where she lives."

"Might she have given the key to anyone else?"

"I don't think she even remembers she *has* a key. We gave it to her years ago, when we first moved in. I don't think she's ever used it."

"Because, you see," Kling said, "there are no marks anywhere. So it's reasonable to assume the man came in with a key."

"Well, I don't think it was Mr. Coe," Angieri said.

"Who?"

"Mr. Coe. The super. He wouldn't do something like this, would he, Marie?"

"No," Mrs. Angieri said.

"I'll talk to him, anyway," Kling said. "The thing is,

there've been twelve burglaries on this same block, and the M.O.'s been the same—the modus operandi—it's been the same in each one, no marks, no signs of entry. So unless there's a ring of burglars who're all building superintendents . . ." Kling smiled. Mrs. Angieri smiled with him. He reminded her of her son, except for the hair. Her son's hair was brown, and Kling's hair was blond. But her son was a big boy, over six feet tall, and so was Kling, and they both had nice boyish smiles. It made her feel a little better about having been robbed.

"I'll need a list of what was taken," Kling said, "and then we'll . . ."

"Is there any chance of getting it back?" Angieri asked.

"Well, that's the thing, you see. We'll get the list out to all the hockshops in the city. Sometimes we get very good results that way. Sometimes, though, the stuff's gotten rid of through a fence, and then it's difficult."

"Well, it isn't likely that he'd take valuable jewelry to a hockshop, is it?"

"Oh, yes, sometimes," Kling said. "But to be honest with you, I think we're dealing with a very high-caliber thief here, and it's my guess he's working with a fence. I could be wrong. And it won't hurt to let the hockshops know what we're looking for."

"Mmm," Angieri said doubtfully.

"I meant to ask you," Kling said. "Was there a kitten?"

"A what?"

"A kitten. He usually leaves a kitten."

"Who does?"

"The burglar."

"Leaves a kitten?"

"Yes. As a sort of calling card. A lot of these thieves are wise guys, you know, they like to think they're making fools of honest citizens. And the police, too."

"Well," Angieri said bluntly, "if he's committed twelve burglaries so far, and you *still* haven't caught him, I guess he *is* making fools of you."

Kling cleared his throat. "But there was no kitten, I gather."

"No kitten."

"He usually leaves it on the bedroom dresser. Tiny little kitten, different one each time. Maybe a month old, something like that."

"Why a kitten?"

"Well, you know, cat burglar, kitten, that's his idea of a joke, I guess. As I said, it's a sort of calling card."

"Mmm," Angieri said again.

"Well," Kling said, "would you like to tell me what's missing, please?"

The superintendent was a black man named Reginald Coe. He told Kling that he had been working here in the building ever since his discharge from the United States Army in 1945. He had fought with the infantry in Italy, which was where he'd got the leg wound that caused his noticeable limp. He now received a pension that, together with his salary as building superintendent, enabled him to provide adequately for his wife and three children. Coe and his family lived in a six-room apartment on the ground floor of the building. It was there that he talked to Kling in the waning hours of the afternoon, both men sipping beer at a spotlessly clean enamel-topped table in the kitchen. In another room of the house the Coe children watched an animated television program, their shrill laughter punctuating the conversation of the two men.

In the Cops-Bending-Over-Backwards Department, Reginald Coe had a great deal going for him. He was black, he was a wounded war veteran, he was a hard-working man, a devoted husband and father, and a genial host. Any cop who did not respond to a man like Coe had to be a racist, a traitor, an ingrate, a loafer, a home wrecker, and a bad guest. Kling tried to be fair in his questioning, but it was really quite impossible to remain unprejudiced. He liked Coe immediately, and knew at once that the man could not have had anything at all to do with the burglary upstairs. But since Coe possessed a duplicate key to the apartment, and since even angelic cherubs have been known to clobber their mothers with hatchets, Kling went through the routine anyway, just so he'd have something to do while drinking the good cold beer.

"Mr. and Mrs. Angieri tell me they left for Jamaica on the twenty-sixth of March. Does that check out with your information, Mr. Coe?"

"That's right," Coe said, nodding. "They caught a late plane Friday night. Told me they were going. So I'd keep an eye on the apartment. I like to know who's in the building and who isn't."

"*Did* you keep an eye on the apartment, Mr. Coe?"

"I did," Coe said, and lifted his beer glass and drank deeply and with obvious satisfaction.

"How?"

"I stopped up there twice."

"When was that?"

"First time on the Wednesday after they left, and again last Wednesday."

"Did you lock the door after you?"

"I did."

"Did it look as if anyone had been in there?"

"Nope. Everything was in its place, all the drawers closed, no mess, no nothing. Not like they found it when they got home last night."

"This was Wednesday, you say? When you were in there?"

"Yes. Last Wednesday."

"That would be the . . ." Kling consulted his pocket calendar. "The seventh of April."

"If that's what it says there. I wouldn't know the exact date."

"Yes, the seventh."

"Then that's when it was," Coe said, and nodded.

"Which means the place was hit sometime between then and last night. Did you see any strangers in the building during that time?"

"No, I didn't. I try to keep a careful eye on what's going on. You get a lot of crooks coming around saying they're repairmen or delivery men, you know, and all they want to do is get in here and carry off anything that ain't nailed down. I watch that very careful. Cop on the beat's a good man, too, knows who lives in the neighborhood and who don't, stops a lot of strangers on the street just to find out what they're up to."

"What's his name, would you know?"

"Mike Ingersoll. He's been on the beat a long time."

"Yes, I know him," Kling said.

"Started here around 1960, sometime around then. He's younger than I am, must be in his late thirties. He's a good cop, been cited for bravery twice. I like him a lot."

"When did you discover the burglary, Mr. Coe?" Kling asked.

"I *didn't* discover it. Everything was all right last time I went in there. Mr. and Mrs. Angieri discovered it when they got home last night. They called the police right off." Coe drank more beer, and then said, "You think this is connected with the other ones on the block?"

"It looks that way," Kling said.

"How do you think he gets in?" Coe asked.

"Through the front door."

"But how?"

"With a key," Kling said.

"You don't think . . ."

"No."

"If you do, Mr. Kling, I wish you'd say so."

"I don't think you had anything to do with this burglary or with any of the others. No, Mr. Coe."

"Good," Coe said. He rose, opened the refrigerator, and, said, "Would you care for another beer?"

"Thank you, I've got to be going."

"It's been nice having you visit," Coe said.

The call from Joseph Angieri came to the squadroom at close to six o'clock that evening, just as Kling was preparing to go home.

"Mr. Kling," he said, "we found the cat."

"I beg your pardon?" Kling said.

"The kitten. You said your man always left a . . ."

"Yes, yes," Kling said. "Where'd you find it?"

"Behind the dresser. Dead. Tiny little thing, gray and white. Must have fallen off and banged its head." Angieri paused. "Do you want me to keep it for you?"

"I don't think so."

"What should I do with it?" Angieri asked.

"Well . . . dispose of it," Kling said.

"Just throw it in the garbage?"

"I suppose so."

"Maybe I'll take it down and bury it in the park."

"Whatever you prefer, Mr. Angieri."

"Tiny little thing," Angieri said. "You know, I happened to remember something after you left."

"What's that?"

"The lock on the front door. We had it changed just before we left for Jamaica. Because of all the burglaries on the block, figured we'd better change the lock. If somebody got in here with a *key*. . ."

"Yes, Mr. Angieri, I follow you," Kling said. "What's the locksmith's name?"

Detective Steve Carella was a tall man with the body and walk of a trained athlete. His eyes were brown, slanting peculiarly downward in an angular face, giving him an oriental appearance that was completely at odds with his Italian background. The downward tilt of the eyes also made him look a trifle mournful at times, again in contradiction to his basically optimistic outlook. He glided toward the ringing telephone now like an outfielder moving up to an easy pop fly, lifted the receiver, sat on the edge of the desk in one fluid motion, and said, "87th Squad, Carella here."

"Have you paid your income tax, Detective Carella?"

This was Friday morning, the sixteenth of April, and Carella had mailed his income tax return on the ninth, a full six days before the deadline. But even though he suspected the caller was Sam Grossman at the lab, or Rollie Chabrier in the D.A.'s office (both of whom were fond of little telephone gags), he nonetheless felt the normal dread of any American citizen when confronted with a voice supposedly originating in the offices of the Internal Revenue Service.

"Yes, I have," he said, carrying it off rather well, he thought. "Who's this, please?"

"No one remembers me anymore," the voice said dolefully. "I'm beginning to feel neglected."

"Oh," Carella said. "It's you."

"Ahh, yes, it's me."

"Detective Meyer mentioned that you'd called. How are you?" Carella said chattily, and signaled to Hal Willis across the room. Willis looked at him in puzzlement. Carella twirled his forefinger as though dialing a phone. Willis nodded, and immediately called the Security Office at the telephone company to ask for a trace on Carella's line, the Frederick 7-8025 extension.

"I'm all right now," the voice said. "I got shot a while back, though. Did you know that, Detective Carella?"

"Yes, I know that."

"In a tailor shop. On Culver Avenue."

"Yes."

"In fact, if I recall correctly, *you're* the man who shot me, Detective Carella."

"Yes, that's my recollection, too." Carella looked at Willis and raised his eyebrows inquisitively. Willis nodded and made an encouraging hand gesture—*keep him talking.*

"Quite painful," the Deaf Man said.

"Yes, getting shot can be painful."

"But then, *you've* been shot, too."

"I have indeed."

"In fact, if I recall correctly, *I'm* the man who shot *you.*"

"With a shotgun, wasn't it?"

"Which makes us even, I suppose."

"Not quite. Getting shot with a shotgun is more painful than getting shot with a pistol."

"Are you trying to trace this call, Detective Carella?"

"How could I? I'm all alone up here."

"I think you're lying," the Deaf Man said, and hung up.

"Get anything?" Carella asked Willis.

"Miss Sullivan?" Willis said into the phone. He listened, shook his head, said, "Thanks for trying," and then hung up. "When's the last time we successfully traced a telephone call?" he asked Carella. He was a short man (the shortest on the squad, in fact, having barely cleared the Department's 5'8" minimum height requirement), with slender hands and the alert brown eyes of a frisky terrier. He walked toward Carella's desk with a bouncing stride, as though he were wearing sneakers.

"He'll call back," Carella said.

"You sounded like two old buddies chatting," Willis said.

"In a sense, we *are* old buddies."

"What do you want me to do if he calls again? Go through the nonsense?"

"No, he's hip to it. He'll never stay on the line more than a few minutes."

"What the hell does he want?" Willis asked.

"Who knows?" Carella answered, and thought about what he'd said just a few moments before. *In a sense, we* are *old buddies.*

He had, he realized, stopped considering the Deaf Man a deadly adversary, and he wondered now how much this had to do with the fact that his wife, Teddy, was a deaf mute. Oddly, he never thought of her as such—except when the Deaf Man put in an appearance. There had never been anything resembling a lack of communication in his relationship with Teddy; her eyes were her ears, and her hands spoke volumes. Teddy was capable of screaming down the roof in pantomime and dismissing his own angry response by simply closing her eyes. Her eyes were brown, almost as dark as her black hair. She watched him intently with those eyes, watched his lips, watched his hands as they moved in the alphabet she had taught him, and which he spoke fluently and with a personality distinctly his own. She was beautiful and passionate and responsive and smart as hell. She was also a deaf mute. But he equated this with the lacy black butterfly she'd had tattooed on her right shoulder more years ago than he could recall; they were both superficial aspects of the woman he loved.

He had once hated the Deaf Man. He no longer did. He had once dreaded his intelligence and nerve. He no longer did. In a curious way he was glad the Deaf Man had returned, but at the same time he sincerely wished the Deaf Man would go away. To return again? It was all very puzzling. Carella sighed and wheeled a typing cart into position near his desk.

From his own desk Willis said, "We don't need him. Not at this time of year. Not with the warm weather starting."

The clock on the squadroom wall read 10:51 A.M.

A half hour had passed since the Deaf Man's last call.

He had not called again, and Carella was not disappointed. As if to support Willis's theory that the Deaf Man was not needed, not with the warm weather starting, the squadroom was now thronged with cops, lawbreakers, and victims—all on a nice quiet Friday morning with the sun shining in a clear blue sky, and the temperature sitting at seventy-two degrees.

There was something about the warm weather that brought them out like cockroaches. The cops of the 87th Precinct rarely enjoyed what could be called a "slow season," but it did appear to them that less crimes were committed during the winter months. During the winter months, it was the firemen who had all the headaches. Slum landlords were not particularly renowned for their generosity in supplying adequate heat to tenement dwellers, despite the edicts of the Board of Health. The apartments in some of the buildings lining the side streets off Culver and Ainsley avenues were only slightly warmer than the nearest igloo. The tenants, coping with rats and faulty electrical wiring and falling plaster and leaking pipes, often sought to bring a little extra warmth into their lives by using cheap kerosene burners that were fire hazards. There were more fires in the 87th Precinct on any given winter's night than in any other part of the city. Conversely, there were less broken heads. It takes a lot of energy to work up passion when you're freezing your ass off. But winter had all but fled the city, and spring was here, and with it came the attendant rites, the celebrations of the earth, the paeans to life and living. The juices were beginning to flow, and nowhere did they flow as exuberantly as in the 87th, where life and death sometimes got a little bit confused and where the flowing juices were all too often a bright red.

The man clinging to the patrolman's arm had an arrow in his chest. They had called for a meat wagon, but in the meantime they didn't know what the hell to do with him. They had never before had a man up here with an arrow sticking in his chest and protruding from his back.

"Why'd you bring him up here?" Willis whispered to the patrolman.

"What'd you want me to do? Leave him wandering around in the park?"

"Yeah, that's what you should have done," Willis whispered. "Let the Department of Hospitals worry about him. This guy can sue us, did you know that? For bringing him up here?"

"He can?" the patrolman whispered, and went immediately pale.

"All right, sit down," Willis said to the man. "Can you hear me? Sit down."

"I got shot," the man said.

"Yeah, yeah, we know that. Now sit down. Will you please sit down? What the hell's the matter with you?"

"I got shot," the man said.

"Who did it?"

"I don't know. Are there Indians in this city?"

"The ambulance is coming," Willis said. "Sit down."

"I want to stand up."

"Why?"

"It hurts more when I sit."

"You're not bleeding much," Willis said softly.

"I know. But it hurts. Did you call the ambulance?"

"I just told you we called the ambulance."

"What time is it?"

"Almost eleven."

"I was taking a walk in the park," the man said. "I felt this sharp pain in my chest, I thought I was having a heart attack. I look down, there's an *arrow* in me."

"All right, sit down, will you, you're making me nervous."

"Is the ambulance coming?"

"It's coming, it's coming."

In the detention cage across the room, a tall blond girl wearing a white blouse and a short tan skirt paced nervously and angrily, and then stepped up to the grilled metal and shouted, "I didn't do nothing, let me out of here."

"The patrolman says you did plenty," Carella said. "You slashed your boyfriend across the face and throat with a razor blade."

"He deserved it," the girl shouted. "Let me out of here."

"We're booking you for first-degree assault," Carella said. "As soon as you calm down, I'm going to take your fingerprints."

"I ain't *never* calming down," the girl shouted.

"We've got all the time in the world."

"You know what I'm going to do?"

"You're going to calm down, and then we're going to take your fingerprints. And then, if you've got any sense, you're going to start praying your boyfriend doesn't die."

"I *hope* he dies. Let me out of here!"

"Nobody's letting you out. Stop yelling, you're busting my ears."

"I'm going to rip off all my clothes and say you tried to rape me."

"Go ahead, we'll enjoy the show."

"You think I'm kidding?"

"Hey, Hal, the girl here's going to take off her clothes."

"Good, let her," Willis said.

"You mother-fuckers," the girl said.

"Nice talk," Carella said.

"You think I won't do it?"

"Do it, who cares?" Carella said, and turned away from the cage to walk toward a patrolman who stood behind two teenage boys handcuffed to each other and to the heavy wooden leg of the fingerprinting table. "What've we got here, Fred?" Carella asked the patrolman.

"Smashed a Cadillac into the window of a grocery store on The Stem. They're both stoned," the patrolman said. "The Caddy was stolen two days ago on the South Side. I've got it on my hot-car list."

"Take off your blouse, honey," one of the boys yelled across the room. "Show us your tits."

"We'll say they jumped you," the other boy yelled, giggling. "Go ahead, baby, do it."

"Anybody injured?" Carella asked the patrolman.

"Nobody in the store but the owner, and he was behind the counter."

"How about it?" Carella asked the boys.

"How about what?" the first boy said. He had long black curly hair and a thick black beard. He was wearing blue jeans and a striped polo shirt over which was a tan windbreaker. He kept looking toward the detention cage, where the girl had begun pacing again.

"You crash that car into the window?"

"What car?" he said.

"The blue Caddy that was stolen from in front of

1604 Stewart Place Wednesday night," the patrolman said.

"You're dreaming," the boy answered.

"Rip off your blouse, honey!" the second boy shouted. He was shorter than his companion, with long stringy brown hair and pale blue eyes. He was wearing tan chinos and a Mexican poncho. He did not have a shirt on under the poncho. He, too, kept watching the detention cage, where the girl had approached the locked door again and was peering owlishly into the room, as though contemplating her next move. "*Do* it!" he shouted to her. "Are you chicken?"

"Shut up, punk," she answered.

"Did you steal that car?" Carella asked.

"I don't know what car you're talking about," the boy said.

"The car you drove through the grocery-store window."

"We weren't driving no car, man," the first boy said.

"We were *flying*, man," the second boy said, and both of them began giggling.

"Better not book them till they know what's going on," Carella said. "Take them down, Fred. Tell Sergeant Murchison they're stoned and won't understand their rights." He turned to the nearest boy and said, "How old are you?"

"Fifty-eight," the boy answered.

"Sixty-five," the second boy said, and again they giggled.

"Take them down," Carella said. "Keep them away from anybody, they may be juveniles."

The patrolman unlocked the cuff holding them to the leg of the table. As he led them toward the slatted railing that divided the squadroom from the corridor, the bearded boy turned toward the detention cage again and shouted, "You got nothing to show, anyway!" and then burst into laughter as the patrolman prodded him from behind with his nightstick.

"You think I won't do it?" the girl again said to Carella.

"Sweetheart, we don't care *what* you do," Carella answered, and walked to Kling's desk, where an old woman sat in a long black overcoat, her hands folded demurely in her lap.

"*Che vergogna,*" the woman said, nodding her head in disapproval of the girl in the cage.

"Yes," Carella answered. "Do you speak English, *signora?*"

"I have been in America forty years."

"Would you like to tell me what happened?"

"Someone steal my pocketbook."

Carella moved a pad into place before him. "What's your name, *signora?*"

"Caterina Di Paolo."

"And your address?"

"Hey, is this a gag?" somebody called from the railing. Carella looked up. A white-suited ambulance attendant was standing there, looking disbelievingly into the squadroom. "Did somebody *really* get shot with an arrow?"

"There he is," Willis said.

"That's an arrow, all right," the attendant said, his eyes bugging.

"Rape, rape!" the girl in the detention cage suddenly shouted, and Carella turned and saw that she had removed her blouse and brassiere.

"Oh, Jesus," he muttered, and then said, "Excuse me, *signora*," and was walking toward the cage when the telephone on his own desk rang.

He lifted the receiver.

"Come on, mister," the ambulance attendant said.

"They ripped off my clothes!" the girl shouted. "Look at me!"

"*Che vergogna,*" the old lady said, and began clucking her tongue.

"With your assistance," the Deaf Man said, "I'm going to steal five hundred thousand dollars on the last day of April."

The manila envelope was addressed in typescript to Detective Steven Louis Carella, 87th Squad, 41 Grover Avenue. There was no return address on the envelope. It had been postmarked in Isola the day before. The picture was inside the envelope, neatly sandwiched between two pieces of gray shirt cardboard.

"That's J. Edgar Hoover, isn't it?" Meyer asked.

"That's who it is," Carella said.

"Why a photograph of him?"

"It isn't even a photograph," Carella said. "It's a photo*stat*."

"Federal government is undoubtedly cutting back on expenses," Meyer said. "Recession, you know."

"Undoubtedly," Carella said.

"What do you think?" Meyer asked seriously.

"I think it's our friend."

"So do I."

"His opening gun."

"Why Hoover?"

"Why not?"

Meyer scratched his bald pate. "What's he trying to tell us, Steve?"

"I haven't the foggiest notion," Carella said.

"Well, figure it out, figure it out."

"Well," Carella said, "he told me yesterday that he plans to steal half a million dollars on the last day of April. So now," he said, and glanced at the wall clock, "at exactly nine twenty-two the next morning, we receive a photostat of J. Edgar Hoover. He's either trying to tell us something, or trying to tell us nothing, or trying to tell us something that means nothing."

"That's brilliant reasoning," Meyer said. "Have you ever thought of going into police work?"

"I'm basing my deduction upon his past M.O. Remember that first job, whenever the hell it was?"

"More than ten years ago."

"Right. He led us to believe he was going to hit one bank when he was really after another. Incidentally, wasn't *that* hit also scheduled for the last day of April?"

"It was."

"And he damn near got away with it."

"Damn near."

"He lets us know what he's planning to do, but he doesn't *really* let us know. It's no fun for him otherwise. Look at what he did on his next job. Announced each of his planned murders beforehand, knocked off two city officials in a row, and threatened to knock off the mayor himself. But only because he was trying to extort money from *other* people, and was using those high-caliber murders as warnings. It's all misdirected direction,

Meyer. Which is why I say this picture can mean everything or it can mean nothing."

Meyer looked at the photostat again. "Hoover," he said blankly.

The locksmith's name was Stanislaw Janik.

His shop was an eight-by-ten cubicle wedged between a hockshop and a dry-cleaning store on Culver Avenue. The wall behind his counter was made of pegboard upon which hung blank keys. Each blank was identified by a code number that corresponded to a similar number in the manufacturer's catalog. In the case of automobile keys, the blanks were coded according to year and make. There were six full-grown cats in the shop. The place stank of cat shit.

Janik himself resembled a cross-eyed Siamese, blue eyes magnified behind bifocals, bald save for a tuft of black hair behind each ear. A man in his early fifties, he sat on a stool behind the counter, wearing a tan sweater over a white shirt open at the throat, cutting a key as Kling came into the shop. The bell over the door tinkled, and a cat who had been lying just behind the door growled angrily and leaped halfway across the room.

"Mr. Janik?" Kling said.

Janik looked up from the key and turned off the duplicating machine. His teeth were nicotine-stained; a Sherlock Holmes pipe rested in an ashtray near the machine. The counter top was covered with brass filings. He brushed them aside with the back of his hand and said, "Yes, can I help you?" His speech was faintly accented; Kling could not place the country of origin. He reached into his pocket, opened his wallet to where his shield was pinned to a leather flap opposite his lucite-encased I.D. card, and said, "Police officer. I'd like to ask you some questions, please."

"What's the matter?" Janik asked.

"I'm investigating some burglaries on Richardson Drive."

"Yes?"

"I understand you installed a lock for one of the burglary victims."

"Who would that be?" Janik asked. A black and white cat leaped suddenly from the floor to the counter and offered its back to Janik. He began stroking the cat idly, not looking at the animal, watching Kling instead from behind his thick spectacles.

"A Mr. Joseph Angieri," Kling said. "At 638 Richardson."

"Yes, I installed a lock for him," Janik said, stroking the cat's arched back.

"What kind of a lock was it?"

"A simple cylinder lock. Not good enough," Janik said, shaking his head.

"What do you mean?"

"I told Mr. Angieri. He was having the lock changed because of the burglaries, do you understand? So I told him this type of cylinder lock was not sufficient protection, that he should allow me to put in a deadlock. Are you familiar with this lock?"

"I am," Kling said.

"It would have been adequate protection. Even if you remove the cylinder on a deadlock, there is a shutter guard that prevents entry. I suggested a Fox lock, too, as an added precaution. If he was afraid of burglary . . ."

"You seem to know a lot about burglary, Mr. Janik."

"Locks are my business," Janik said, and shrugged. He pushed the cat off the counter. Startled, the cat landed on the floor, scowled up at him, stretched, and stalked off into the corner, where it began licking the ear of a tan Angora. "I told Mr. Angieri that the little extra money would be worth it. For the deadlock I mean. He said no, he wasn't interested in that kind of investment. So now his place is broken into. So he saved a little money on a cheaper lock, and he lost all his valuable possessions. What kind of thrift is that? Senseless," Janik said, and shook his head again.

"Would you have any idea what his loss was, Mr. Janik?"

"None."

"Then . . . why do you say he lost valuable possessions?"

"I assume if someone breaks into an apartment, it is not to open a piggy bank and steal a few pennies. What are you trying to say, young man?"

"Have you installed locks for anyone else in this neighborhood, Mr. Janik?"

"As I told you before, locks are my business. Of *course* I have installed other locks in the neighborhood. My *shop* is in the neighborhood, where would you expect me to install locks? In California?"

"Have you installed other locks on Richardson Drive?"

"I have."

"Where on Richardson Drive? Which apartments?"

"I would have to consult my records."

"Would you please?"

"No, I would not."

"Mr. Janik . . ."

"I don't believe I care for your manner, young man. I'm very busy, and I don't have time to go through my bills to see just which apartments had locks installed by me. I ask you again, what are you trying to say?"

"Mr. Janik . . ." Kling said, and hesitated.

"Yes?"

"Would you happen to have duplicate keys for the locks you've installed?"

"I would not. Are you suggesting I'm a thief?"

"No, sir. I merely . . ."

"I came to this country from Poland in 1948. My wife and children were killed by the Germans, and I am alone in the world. I earn a meager living, but I earn it honestly. Even in Poland, when I was starving, I never stole so much as a crust of bread. I am not a thief, young man, and I do not choose to show you my bills. I will thank you to leave my shop."

"I may be back, Mr. Janik."

"You are free to return. Provided you come with a warrant. I have had enough of storm troopers in my lifetime."

"I'm sure you understand, Mr. Janik . . ."

"I understand nothing. Please go."

"Thank you," Kling said, and walked to the door. He turned, started to say something else, and then opened the door instead. The bell tinkled, and one of the cats almost ran out onto the sidewalk. Kling hastily closed the door behind him and began walking the six blocks to the station house. He felt he had handled the whole thing badly. He felt like a goddamn Nazi. It was a bright spring day, and the air was clean and fresh, but the stink of cat shit lingered in his nostrils.

• • •

At 3:30 P.M., fifteen minutes before Kling was supposed to be relieved, the phone on his desk rang. He picked it up and said:

"87th Squad, Kling."

"Bert, this is Murchison on the desk. Just got a call from Patrolman Ingersoll at 657 Richardson Drive. He's in 11D with a lady who just got back from a trip abroad. The apartment's been ripped off."

"I'll get right over there," Kling said.

He walked to where Hal Willis was sitting at his own desk, two dozen forged checks spread out before him, and said, "Hal, I've got another burglary on Richardson. I'll probably head straight home from there."

"Right," Willis said, and went back to comparing the signatures on the checks against a suspect signature on a motel registration card. "This guy's been hanging paper all over town," he said conversationally, without looking up.

"Did you hear me?" Kling asked.

"Yeah, burglary on Richardson, heading straight home," Willis said.

"See you," Kling said, and went out of the squadroom. His car was illegally parked on Grover, two blocks from the station house. The visor on the driver's side was down and a hand-lettered sign clipped to it read: POLICE DEPARTMENT VEHICLE. Each time he came back to it at the end of his tour he expected to find it decorated with a parking citation from some overzealous uniformed cop. He checked the windshield now, unlocked the door, shoved the visor up, and drove over to Richardson, where he double-parked alongside a tobacco-brown Mercedes-Benz. He told the doorman he was a police officer, and explained where he had left the car. The doorman promised to call him in apartment 11D if the owner of the Mercedes wanted to get out.

Mike Ingersoll opened the door on Kling's second ring. He was a handsome cop in his late thirties, slightly older than Kling, with curly black hair, brown eyes, and a nose as straight and as swift as a machete slash. He looked in his uniform the way a lot of patrolmen *thought* they looked, but didn't. He wore it with casual pride, as though it had been tailored exclusively for him in a fancy shop on Hall Avenue, rather than picked off a ready-to-wear rack in a store across the street from the Police Academy downtown. "You got here fast," he said to Kling, and stepped out of the doorway to let him in. His voice, in contrast to his size, was quite soft and came as a distinct surprise; one expected something fuller and rounder to rumble up out of his barrel chest. "Lady's in the living room," be said. "Place is a complete mess. The guy really cleaned her out."

"Same one?"

"I think so. No marks on the windows or door, a white kitten on the bedroom dresser."

"Well," Kling said, and sighed. "Let's talk to the lady."

The lady was sitting on the living-room sofa.

The lady had long red hair and green eyes and a deep suntan. She was wearing a dark green sweater, a short brown skirt, and brown boots. Her legs crossed, she kept staring at the wall as Kling came into the room, and then turned to face him. His first impression was one of total harmony, a casual perfection of color and design, russet and green, hair and eyes, sweater and skirt, boots blending with the smoothness of her tan, the long sleek grace of crossed legs, the inquisitively angled head, the red hair cascading in clean vertical descent. Her face and figure came as residuals to his brief course in art appreciation. High cheekbones, eyes slanting up from them, fiercely green against the tan, tilted nose gently drawing the upper lip away from partially exposed, even white teeth. Her sweater swelled over breasts firm without a bra, the wool cinched tightly at her waist with a brown, brass-studded belt, hip softly carving an arc against the nubby sofa back, skirt revealing a secret thigh as she turned more fully toward him.

He had never seen a more beautiful woman in his life.

"I'm Detective Kling," he said. "How do you do?"

"Hullo," she said dully. She seemed on the edge of tears. Her green eyes glistened, she extended her hand to him, and he took it clumsily, and they exchanged handshakes, and he could not take his eyes from her face. He realized all at once that he was still holding her hand. He dropped it abruptly, cleared his throat, and reached into his pocket for his pad.

"I don't believe I have your name, miss," he said.

"Augusta Blair," she said. "Did you see the mess inside? In the bedroom?"

"I'll take a look in a minute," Kling said. "When did you discover the theft, Miss Blair?"

"I got home about half an hour ago."

"From where?"

"Austria."

"Nice thing to come home to," Ingersoll said, and shook his head.

"Was the door locked when you got here?" Kling asked.

"Yes."

"You used your key to get in?"

"Yes."

"Anybody in the apartment?"

"No."

"Did you hear anything? Any sound at all?"

"Nothing."

"Tell me what happened."

"I came in, and I left the door open behind me because I knew the doorman was coming up with my bags. Then I took off my coat and hung it in the hall closet, and then I went to the john, and then I went into the bedroom. Everything looked all right until then. The minute I stepped in there, I felt . . . invaded."

"You'd better take a look at it, Bert," Ingersoll said. "The guy went sort of berserk."

"That it?" Kling asked, indicating a doorway across the room.

"Yes," Augusta said, and rose from the couch. She was a tall girl, at least five-seven, perhaps five-eight, and she moved with swift grace, preceding him to the bedroom door, looking inside once again, and then turning away in dismay. Kling went into the room, but she did not follow him. She stood in the doorframe instead, worrying her lip, her shoulder against the jamb.

The burglar had slashed through the room like a hurricane. The dresser drawers had all been pulled out and dumped onto the rug—slips, bras, panties, sweaters, stockings, scarves, blouses, spilling across the room in a dazzle of color. Similarly, the clothes on hangers had been yanked out of the closet and flung helter-skelter—coats, suits, skirts, gowns, robes strewn over the floor, bed, and chairs. A jewelry box had been overturned in the center of the bed, and bracelets, rings, beads, pendants, chokers glittered amid a swirl of chiffon, silk, nylon, and wool. A white kitten sat on the dresser top, mewing.

"Did he find what he was looking for?" Kling asked.

"Yes," she answered. "My good jewelry was wrapped in a red silk scarf at the back of the top drawer. It's gone."

"Anything else?"

"Two furs. A leopard and an otter."

"He's selective," Ingersoll said.

"Mmm," Kling said. "Any radios, phonographs, stuff like that?"

"No. The hi-fi equipment's in the living room. He didn't touch it."

"I'll need a list of the jewelry and coats, Miss Blair."

"What for?"

"Well, so we can get working on it. Also, I'm sure you want to report this to your insurance company."

"None of it was insured."

"Oh, boy," Kling said.

"I just never thought anything like this would happen," Augusta said.

"How long have you been *living* here?" Kling asked incredulously.

"The city or the apartment?"

"Both."

"I've lived in the city for a year and a half. The apartment for eight months."

"Where are you from originally?"

"Seattle."

"Are you presently employed?" Kling said, and took out his pad.

"Yes."

"Can you give me the name of the firm?"

"I'm a model," Augusta said. "I'm represented by the Cutler Agency."

"Were you in Austria on a modeling assignment?"

"No, vacation. Skiing."

"I thought you looked familiar," Ingersoll said. "I'll bet I've seen your picture in the magazines."

"Mmm," Augusta said without interest.

"How long were you gone?" Kling asked.

"Two weeks. Well, sixteen days, actually."

"Nice thing to come home to," Ingersoll said again, and again shook his head.

"I moved here because it had a doorman," Augusta said. "I thought buildings with doormen were safe."

"*None* of the buildings on this side of the city are safe," Ingersoll said.

"Not many of them, anyway," Kling said.

"I couldn't afford anything across the park," Augusta said. "I haven't been modeling a very long time, I don't really get many bookings." She saw the question on Kling's face and said, "The furs were gifts from my mother, and the jewelry was left to me by my aunt. I saved six goddamn months for the trip to Austria," she said, and suddenly burst into tears. "Oh, shit," she said, "why'd he have to do this?"

Ingersoll and Kling stood by awkwardly. Augusta turned swiftly, walked past Ingersoll to the sofa, and took a handkerchief from her handbag. She noisily blew her nose, dried her eyes, and said, "I'm sorry."

"If you'll let me have the complete list . . ." Kling said.

"Yes, of course."

"We'll do what we can to get it back."

"Sure," Augusta said, and blew her nose again.

Everybody figured it was a mistake.

They were naturally grateful (who wouldn't be?) to receive a second photostated picture of the late beloved leader of our nation's finest security force, but they could not see any reason for it, and so they automatically figured somebody had goofed. It was unlike the Deaf Man to say anything twice when once would suffice. Nor was there any question but that the photostats were identical. The only difference between the one that had arrived in the mail on Saturday, April 17, and the one that arrived today, April 19, were the postmarks on the envelopes. But aside from that, everything was the same, an obvious error. The boys of the 87th were beginning to feel more cheerful about the entire matter; perhaps the Deaf Man was getting senile.

There were five pages of listings for photostat shops in the yellow pages of the Isola directory alone, and perhaps the police should have begun contacting each, on the off chance that one of them had copied Hoover's picture. But nobody was forgetting that thus far no crime had been committed; you could not go around wasting the time of civil servants unless there was something that might conceivably justify such expense. One could, of course, argue that the Deaf Man's past murderous exploits were reason enough for mobilizing the entire police department, getting those men out checking shops, clerks making telephone calls, mailing flyers, and so on. Conversely, one could just as reasonably argue that nobody really knew whether the two pictures of Hoover had indeed come from the Deaf Man, or whether they were in any way linked with the crime he had said he would commit. Given an overworked, understaffed police force with other pressing matters to worry about—like muggings, knifings, shootings, holdups, rapes, burglaries, forgeries, car thefts, oh you know, nuisance stuff—it was perhaps understandable why the cops of the 87th merely asked the laboratory whether the printing paper was unique and whether or not there were any good latent prints on it. The answers to both questions were depressing. The paper was garden-variety crap, and there were no latent prints on it, good or otherwise.

And then, because police work is not all fun and games and looking at pretty pictures, they got to work on a squeal that came in at 10:27 that morning.

The young man had been nailed to the tenement wall.

Long-haired, with a handlebar mustache, wearing only undershorts, he hung like a latter-day Christ bereft of wooden crucifix, a knife wound on the left side of his chest just below the heart, his arms widespread, a spike driven into the wall through each open palm, legs crossed and impaled with a third large spike, head lolling to the side. A vagrant wino had stumbled upon the body, but there was no telling how long he had been hanging there. The blood no longer ran from his wounds. He had soiled himself either in fright or in death, and his own rank stench mingled with the putrid stink of garbage in the empty room so that the detectives turned away from the open doorframe and went out into the corridor, where the air was only slightly less fetid.

The building was one in a long row of abandoned tenements on North Harrison, infested with rats, inhabited for a time by hippies, discarded by them later when they discovered it was too easy to be victimized there by men and beasts alike. The word LOVE still decorated a wall in the hallway, painted flowers running rampant around it in a faded circle, but the dead man in the empty room stank of his own excrement, and the assistant medical examiner did not want to go in to examine the corpse.

"Why should I get all the bad ones?" he asked Carella. "All the jobs nobody else wants, I get. The hell with it. He can rot in there, for all I care. Let the hospital people take him down and cart him to the morgue. We'll examine him there, where at least I can wash my hands afterwards."

The ceiling above their heads was bloated with water, the plaster dangerously loose and close to falling. The room in which the boy hung dead and crucified had one shattered window, and no door in its frame. It had been used as a makeshift garbage dump by the building's squatters, and the garbage was piled three feet high, a thick carpet of moldering food, rusting cans, broken bottles, newspapers, used condoms, and animal feces, topped, as though with a maraschino cherry, with a swollen dead rat. For anyone to have entered the room, it would have been necessary to climb *up* onto the ledge formed by the garbage. The ceiling was perhaps twelve feet high, and the man's impaled feet were crossed some six inches above the line of garbage. He was a tall young man. Whoever had driven the spikes through his extended hands had been even taller, but the body had sagged of its own weight since, dislocating both shoulders and wreaking God knew what internal damage.

"You hear me?" the M.E. said.

"Do what you like," Carella answered.

"I will."

"Just make sure we get a full necropsy report."

"You think he was alive when they nailed him there?" Meyer asked.

"Maybe. The stabbing may have been an afterthought," Carella said.

"I'm not taking him down, and that's that," the M.E. said.

"Look," Carella said angrily, "take him down, leave him there, it's up to you. Send us your goddamn report, and don't forget prints."

"I won't."

"Footprints, too."

"More crazy bastards in this city," the M.E. said, and walked off sullenly, picking his way through the rubble in the corridor, and starting down the staircase to the street, where he hoped to sell his case to the ambulance people when they arrived.

"Let's check the rest of the floor," Meyer said.

There were two other apartments on the floor. The

locks on the doors to both had been broken. In one apartment there were the remains of a recent fire in the center of the room. A worn tennis sneaker was in the corner near the window. Meyer lifted it with his handkerchief, and then bagged and tagged it for transportation to the lab. The second room was empty except for a soiled and torn mattress covered with rat leavings.

"What a shit hole," someone said behind them, and Meyer and Carella turned to find Detective Monoghan in the doorway. Detective Monroe was immediately behind him. Both Homicide cops had gray fedoras on their heads, black topcoats on their backs, and pained expressions on their faces.

"People actually *live* in these shit holes, can you imagine that?" Monroe said.

"Incredible," Monoghan said, wagging his head.

"Unbelievable," Monroe said.

"Where's the stiff?" Monoghan asked.

"Down the hall," Carella said.

"Want to show me?"

"You'll find it," Carella answered.

"Come on," Monoghan said to his partner, and both of them went down the hallway, big-shouldered men pushing their way through the empty corridor as though dispersing a crowd. "Holy mother of God!" Monoghan said.

Carella nodded.

There were footfalls on the steps. Two men in white picked their way over fallen plaster and lath, looked up when they reached the landing, saw Carella, and walked to him immediately.

"Listen, are you in charge here?" one of them asked.

"It's my case, yes," Carella said.

"I'm Dr. Cortez, what's this about wanting *me* to get somebody off the wall?"

"He's got to be taken to the mortuary," Carella said.

"Fine, we'll get him to the mortuary. But your medical examiner says he's *nailed* to the goddamn wall. I don't . . ."

"That's right."

"*I* don't plan to take him down, pal."

"Who do you suggest for the job, pal?" Carella asked.

"I don't *care* who. You look strong enough, why don't you handle it yourself?"

"That's a murder victim in there," Carella said flatly.

"That's a corpse in there," Cortez answered, equally flatly.

Monoghan was coming back down the corridor, holding his nose. Monroe was a step behind him, his hand cupped over the lower part of his face.

"These men are from Homicide," Carella said. "Talk to them about it."

"Who's supposed to take down the corpse?" Cortez asked.

"The M.E. through with it?" Monoghan said.

"He won't examine it here," Carella said.

"He's *got* to examine it here. Those are regulations. We can't move the body till the M.E. examines it, pronounces it dead, and . . ."

"Yeah, go tell that to *him*," Cortez said.

"Where is he?" Monoghan asked.

"Downstairs. Puking out his guts."

"Come on," Monoghan said to his partner, and they headed for the staircase. "You wait here, Carella."

They listened to the two Homicide cops making their

way downstairs. Their footfalls died. There was a strained silence in the corridor.

"Listen, I'm sorry I got so snotty," Cortez said.

"That's okay," Carella answered.

"But he knows the regulations as well as I do. He's just trying to get out of a messy job, that's all."

"Um-huh," Carella said.

"He knows the regulations," Cortez repeated.

The assistant medical examiner, if he had not previously known the regulations, knew them letter-perfect by the time Monoghan and Monroe got through with him downstairs. With a handkerchief tied over his nose, and wearing rubber gloves, he took down the impaled body of the unidentified white male, and performed a cursory examination before declaring him officially dead.

Everybody could now begin tackling the *next* unpleasant task of finding out who had made him that way.

Detective Cotton Hawes looked at the photostat that came in Tuesday morning's mail and decided it was General George Washington.

"Who does that look like to you?" he asked Miscolo, who had come out of the Clerical Office to pick up the weekend's D.D. reports for filing.

"Napoleon Bonaparte," Miscolo said dryly. Shaking his head, he went out of the squadroom muttering. Hawes *still* thought it looked like Washington.

He had been filled in on the latest activities of the Deaf Man, and he assumed now that the photostat was intended as a companion piece to the pictures of J. Edgar Hoover. He immediately connected Hoover and Washington in the obviously logical way—the main office of the Federal Bureau of Investigation was in the city of Washington, D.C. Hoover, Washington, simple. When dealing with the Deaf Man, however, nothing was simple; Hawes recoiled from his first thought as though bitten by it. If the Deaf Man's planned crime was to take place in Washington, he would not be pestering the hard-working cops (Oh, how hard they worked!) of the 87th. Instead, he would be cavorting on the Mall, taunting the cops of the District of Columbia, those stalwarts. No. This picture of the father of the country was meant to indicate something more than the name of a city, Hawes was certain of that. He was equally certain that J. Edgar's fine face was meant to represent something more than the name of a vacuum cleaner, splendid product though it was. He suddenly wondered what the "J." stood for. James? Jack? Jerome? Jules?

"Alf!" he shouted, and Miscolo, down the corridor in the Clerical Office, yelled, "Yo?"

"Come in here a minute, will you?"

Hawes rose from behind his desk and held the picture of Washington out at arm's length. Hawes was a big man, six feet two inches tall, weighing 190 pounds, give or take a few for sweets or pizza. He had a straight unbroken nose, a good mouth with a wide lower lip, and red hair streaked with white over the left temple, where he had once been knifed by a building superintendent who had mistaken him for a burglar. His eyes were blue, and his vision had been as sharp as a hatpin when he'd joined the force. But that was many years ago, and we all begin to show the signs of age, sonny. He held the picture at arm's length now because he was a trifle far-sighted and not at all certain that Miscolo *hadn't* identified it correctly.

No, it was Washington, all right, no question about it.

"It's Washington," he said to Miscolo as he came into the squadroom carrying a sheaf of papers.

"You don't say?" Miscolo said dryly. He looked harried, and hardly in the mood for small talk. Hawes debated asking his question, figured What the hell, and plunged ahead regardless.

"What does the 'J.' in J. Edgar Hoover stand for?"

"John," Miscolo said.

"Are you sure?"

"I'm positive."

"John," Hawes said.

"John," Miscolo repeated.

The two men looked at each other.

"Is that all?" Miscolo asked.

"Yes, thanks a lot, Alf."

"Don't mention it," Miscolo, said. Shaking his head, he went out of the squadroom muttering.

John Edgar Hoover, Hawes thought. John. And George, of course. Names fascinated him. He himself had been named after the fiery Puritan preacher Cotton Mather. Hawes had never felt comfortable with the name and had debated changing it legally some ten years ago, when he was going with a Jewish girl named Rebecca Gold. The girl had said, "If you change your name, Cotton, I'll never go out with you again." Puzzled, he had asked, "But why, Rebecca?" and she had answered, "Your name's the only thing I like about you." He had stopped seeing her the next week.

He still thought wistfully of what he might have become—a Cary Hawes, or a Paul, or a Carter, or a Richard. But more than any of those, the name he most cherished (and he had never revealed this to a soul) was Lefty. Lefty Hawes. Was there a criminal anywhere in the world who would not tremble at the very mention of that dread name, Lefty Hawes? Even though he was right-handed? Hawes thought not. Sighing, he moved the picture of the first President so that it was directly below him on the desk top. Fiercely, he stared into those inscrutable eyes, challenging them to reveal the Deaf Man's secret. Washington never so much as blinked back. Hawes stretched, yawned, picked up the photostat, and carried it to Carella's desk, where it would be waiting when he got back to the office.

The tall blond man, hearing aid in his right ear, came through the revolving doors of the bank at fifteen minutes before noon. He was wearing a custom-tailored beige gabardine suit, an oatmeal-colored shirt, a dark brown tie, brown socks, and brown patent leather shoes. He knew from his previous visits to the bank that there were cameras focused on the area just inside the revolving doors, and cameras covering the five tellers' cages on the left as well. The cameras, if they operated like most bank cameras he had investigated, took a random picture once every thirty seconds, and did not begin taking consecutive and continuous frames for a motion picture unless activated by a teller or some other member of the bank's staff. He had no fear of his picture being taken, however, since he was a bona-fide depositor here on legitimate business.

He had been here for the first time a month ago, on legitimate business, to deposit $5,000 into a new savings account that paid 5 percent interest if the money was not withdrawn before the expiration of ninety days. He had assured the assistant manager that he had no intention of withdrawing the money before that time. He had been lying. He had *every* intention of withdrawing his $5,000, plus $495,000 more, on the last day of April. But his visit to the bank had been legitimate.

On two occasions last week, he had again visited the bank on legitimate business—to make small deposits in the newly opened account. Today, he was here on further legitimate business—to deposit $64 into the account. In addition, he was here to determine exactly how he would deploy his task force of five on the day of the robbery.

The bank guard stood just inside the revolving doors, at almost the exact focal point of the camera on the left. He was a man in his sixties, somewhat paunchy, a retired mailroom clerk or messenger who wore his uniform with shabby authority and who would probably drop dead of fright if he was ever forced to pull the .38 caliber revolver holstered at his side. He smiled at the Deaf Man as he came into the bank, his patent leather shoes clicking on the marbled floors. The Deaf Man returned the smile, his back to the camera that angled down from the ledge on the right of the entrance doors. Immediately ahead of him were two marble-topped tables secured to the floor and compartmentalized below their counters to accommodate checking-account deposit slips and savings-account withdrawal and deposit slips. He walked to the nearest table, stood on the side of it opposite the tellers' cages, and began a quick drawing.

Looking into the bank from the entrance, there were three cages on the right side. He stood facing those cages now, his back turned to the clerical office and the loan department. Angling off from these, and running across the entire rear wall of the bank, was the vault, its shining steel door open now, its body encased in concrete and steel mesh interlaced with wires for the alarm system.

There was no feasible way of approaching that vault from above it, below it, or behind it. The assault would have to be head-on, but not without its little diversions.

Smiling, the Deaf Man considered the diversions. Or, to be more accurate, the *single* diversion that would ensure the success of the robbery. To say that he considered the police antiquated and foolish would have been unfair to the enormity of his disdain; in fact, be considered them obsolete and essentially hebephrenic. Paradoxically, the success of his scheme depended upon at least some measure of intelligence on the part of his adversaries, so he was making it as simple as he could for them, spelling it out in pictures because he sensed words might be too confusing. He had begun explaining exactly where and when he would strike, and he had played fair and would continue to play fair; cheating the police would have been the equivalent of tripping a cripple in a soccer match. Although he suspected himself of sadistic tendencies, he could best exorcise those in bed with a willing wench rather than take advantage of the bumbleheads who worked in the 87th Precinct. He looked upon them almost fondly, like cretinous children who needed to be taken to the circus every now and then. In fact, he rather liked the concept of himself as a circus, complete with clowns and lion-taming acts and high-wire excitement, a one-man circus come to set the city on its ear again.

But in order for the diversion to work, in order for the spectator's eye to become captured by the prancing ponies in the center ring while man-eating tigers consumed their trainer in the third ring, the diversion had to be plain and evident. The key to his brilliant scheme (he admitted this modestly), the code he had concocted, was simple to comprehend. Too simple? No, he did not think so. They would learn from the photostats only what he wanted them to learn; they would see only the ponies and miss the Bengal tigers. And then, thrilled with their own perception, inordinately proud of having been able to focus on the flashing hoofs, they would howl in pain when bitten on the ass from behind. All fair and above board. All there for the toy police to see, if only they were capable of seeing, if only they possessed the brains of gnats or the imagination of rivets.

The Deaf Man finished his floor plan of the bank. He folded the deposit slip as though he had been making money calculations in the secret manner of bank depositors everywhere, put it into his pocket, and then took another slip from the rack. He quickly filled it out, and walked to the nearest teller's cage.

"Good morning, sir," the teller said, and smiled pleasantly.

"Good morning," the Deaf Man said, and returned the smile. Bored, he watched as the teller went about the business of recording the deposit. There were alarm buttons on the floor behind each of the tellers' cages and scattered elsewhere throughout the bank. They did not overly concern him.

The Deaf Man thought it fitting that a police detective would help him rob the bank.

He also thought it fitting that the police detective who would lend his assistance was Steve Carella.

Things had a way of interlocking neatly if one bided his time and played his cards according to the laws of permutation and combination.

"Here you are, sir," the teller said, and handed back the passbook. The Deaf Man perfunctorily checked the entry, nodded, slipped the book back into its plastic carrying case, and walked toward the revolving doors. He nodded at the security guard, who politely nodded back, and then he went into the street outside.

The bank was a mile outside the 87th Precinct territory, not far from three large factories on the River Harb. McCormick Container Corp. employed 6,347 people. Meredith Mints, Inc. employed 1,512. Holt Brothers, Inc. employed 4,048 for a combined work force of close to twelve thousand and a combined payroll of almost $2 million a week. These weekly salaries were paid by check, with roughly 40 percent of the personnel electing to have the checks mailed directly to banks of their own choice. Of the remaining 60 percent, half took their checks home to cash in supermarkets, whiskey stores, department stores, and/or banks in their own neighborhoods. But some 30 percent of the combined work force of the three plants cashed their checks each and every week at the bank the Deaf Man had just visited. Which meant that every Friday the bank *expected* to cash checks totaling approximately $600,000. In order to meet this anticipated weekly drain, the bank supplemented its own cash reserve with money shipped from its main branch. This money, somewhere in the vicinity of $500,000, depending on what cash the bank already had on hand, was delivered by armored truck at nine-fifteen each Friday morning. There were three armed guards on the truck. One guard stayed behind the wheel while the other two, revolvers drawn, went into the bank carrying two sacks of cash. The manager accompanied them into the vault, where they deposited the money, and then left the bank, revolvers now holstered. At eleven-thirty the cash was distributed to the tellers in anticipation of the lunch-hour rush of factory workers seeking to cash their salary checks.

The Deaf Man had no intention of intercepting the truck on its way from the main branch bank. Nor did he wish to hit any one of the individual tellers' cages. No, he wanted to get that money while it was still neatly stacked in the vault. And whereas his own plan was far less dangerous than sticking up an armored truck, he nonetheless felt it to be more audacious. In fact, he considered it innovative to the point of genius, and was certain it would go off without a hitch. Ah yes, he thought, the bank will be robbed, the bank will be robbed, and his step quickened, and he breathed deeply of the heady spring air.

The tennis sneaker found in the abandoned building was in shabby condition, a size-twelve gunboat that had seen better days when it was worn on someone's left foot. The sole was worn almost through in one spot, and the canvas top had an enormous hole near the area of the big toe. Even the laces were weary, having been knotted together after breaking in two spots. The brand name was well-known, which excluded the possibility of the sneaker having been purchased (as part of a pair, naturally) in any exotic boutique. The only thing of possible interest about this left-footed sneaker, in fact, was a brown stain on the tip of it, near the small toe. This was identified by the Police Laboratory as microcrystalline wax, a synthetic the color and consistency of beeswax, but much less expensive. A thin metallic dust adhered to the wax; it was identified as bronze. Carella was not particularly overjoyed by what the lab delivered. Nor was he thrilled by the report from the Identification Section, which had been unable to find any fingerprints, palm prints, or footprints that matched the dead man's. Armed with a somewhat unflattering photograph (it had been taken while the man lay stone-cold dead on a slab at the morgue), Carella went back to the Harrison Street neighborhood that afternoon and tried to find someone who had known him.

The Medical Examiner had estimated the man's age as somewhere between twenty and twenty-five. In terms of police investigation, this was awkward. He could have been running with a younger crowd of teenagers, or an older crowd of young adults, depending on his emotional maturity. Carella decided to try a sampling of each, and his first stop was a teenage coffee house called Space, which had over the years run the gamut from kosher delicatessen to Puerto Rican *bodega* to store-front church to its present status. In contradiction to its name, Space was a ten-by-twelve room with a huge silver espresso machine on a counter at its far end. Like a futuristic idol, the machine intimidated the room and seemed to dwarf its patrons. All of the patrons were young. The girls were wearing blue jeans and long hair. The boys were bearded. In terms of police investigation, this was awkward. It meant they could be (a) hippies, (b) college students, (c) anarchists, (d) prophets, (e) all of the foregoing. To many police officers, of course, long hair or a beard (or both) automatically meant that any person daring to look like that was guilty of (a) possession of marijuana, (b) intent to sell heroin, (c) violation of the Sullivan Act, (d) fornication with livestock, (e) corrupting the morals of a minor, (f) conspiracy, (g) treason, (h) all of the foregoing. Carella wished he had a nickel for every clean-shaven, crew-cutted kid he had arrested for murdering his own brother. On the other hand, he was a police officer and he knew that the moment he showed his badge in this place, these long-haired youngsters would automatically assume he was guilty of (a) fascism, (b) brutality, (c) drinking beer and belching, (d) fornication with livestock, (e) harassment, (f) all of the foregoing. Some days, it was very difficult to earn a living.

The cop smell seeped into the room almost before the door closed behind him. The kids looked at him, and he looked back at them, and he knew that if he asked them what time it was, they would answer in chorus, "The thirty-fifth of December." He chose the table closest to the door, pulling out a chair and sitting between a boy with long blond hair and a dark boy with a straggly beard. The girl opposite him had long brown hair, frightened brown eyes, and the face of an angel.

"Yes?" the blond boy asked.

"I'm a police officer," Carella said, and showed his shield. The boys glanced at it without interest. The girl brushed a strand of hair from her cheek and turned her head away. "I'm trying to identify a man who was murdered in this area."

"When?" the boy with the beard asked.

"Sunday night. April eighteenth."

"Where?" the blond boy asked.

"In an abandoned tenement on Harrison."

"What'd you say your name was?" the blond boy asked.

"Detective Steve Carella."

The girl moved her chair back, and rose suddenly, as

though anxious to get away from the table. Carella put his hand on her arm and said, "What's *your* name, miss?"

"Mary Margaret," she said. She did not sit again. She moved her arm, freeing it from Carella's hand, and then turned to go.

"No last name?" he said.

"Ryan," she said. "See you guys," she said to the boys, and this time moved several paces from the table before she was stopped again by Carella's voice.

"Miss Ryan, would you look at this picture, please?" he said, and removed the photo from his notebook. The girl came back to the table, looked at the picture, and said nothing.

"Does he look familiar?" Carella asked.

"No," she said. "See you," she said again, and this time she walked swiftly from the table and out into the street.

Carella watched her going, and then handed the photograph to the blond boy. "How about you?"

"Nope."

"What's your name?"

"Bob."

"Bob what?"

"Carmody."

"And yours?" he asked the boy with the beard.

"Hank Scaffale."

"You both live in the neighborhood?"

"On Porter Street."

"Have you been living here long?"

"Awhile."

"Are you familiar with most of the people in the neighborhood?"

"The freaks, yeah," Hank said. "I don't have much to do with others."

"Have *you* ever seen this man around?"

"Not if he really looked like that," Hank said, studying the photo.

"What do you mean?"

"He's dead in that picture, isn't he?"

"Yes."

"Yeah, well, that makes a difference," Hank said. "The juices are gone," he said, and shook his head. "All the juices are gone." He studied the photograph again, and again shook his head. "I don't know who he is," he said, "poor bastard."

The responses from the other young people in the room were similar. Carella took the photograph around to the five other tables, explained what he was looking for, and waited while the dead man's frozen image was passed from hand to hand. None of the kids were overly friendly (you can get hit on the head by cops only so often before you decide there may not be a basis there for mutual confidence and trust), but neither were they impolite. They all looked solemnly at the picture, and they all reported that they had not known the dead man. Carella thanked them for their time and went out into the street again.

By five o'clock that afternoon he had hit in succession two head shops, a macrobiotic food store, a record store, a store selling sandals, and four other places catering to the neighborhood's young people—or at least those young people who wore their hair long. He could not bring himself to call them "freaks" despite their apparent preference for the word; to his way of thinking, that was the same as putting an identifying tag on a dead man's toe before you knew who he was. Labels annoyed him unless they were affixed to case report folders or bottles in a medicine cabinet. "Freaks" was a particularly distressing label, demeaning and misleading, originally applied from without, later adopted from within in self-defense, and finally accepted with pride as a form of self-identification. But how in hell did this in any way lessen its derogatory intent? It was the same as cops proudly calling themselves "pigs" in the hope that the epithet would lose its vilifying power once it was exorcised by voluntary application. Bullshit. Carella was not a pig, and the kids he'd spoken to this afternoon were not freaks.

They were young people in a neighborhood as severely divided as any war-torn Asian countryside. In the days when the city was young, or at least younger, the neighborhood population had been mostly immigrant Jewish, with a dash of Italian or Irish thrown in to keep the pot boiling. It boiled a lot in those days (ask Meyer Meyer, who lived in a similar ghetto as a boy, and who was chased through the streets by bigots shouting, "Meyer Meyer, Jew on fire!"), and eventually simmered down to a sort of armed truce between the old-timers, whose children went to college or learned New World trades and moved out to Riverhead or Calm's Point. The next wave of immigrants to hit the area were United States citizens who did not speak the language and who enjoyed all the rights and privileges of any minority group in the city; that is to say, they were underpaid, overcharged, beaten, scorned, and generally made to feel that Puerto Rico was not a beautiful sun-washed island in the Caribbean but rather a stink hole on the outskirts of a smelly swamp. They learned very rapidly that it was all right to throw garbage from the windows into the backyard, because if you didn't the rats would come into the apartment to eat it. Besides, if people are treated like garbage themselves, they cannot be castigated for *any* way they choose to handle their own garbage. The Puerto Ricans came, and some of them stayed only long enough to earn plane fare back to the island. Some followed the immigration pattern established by the Europeans: they learned the language, they went to school, they got better jobs, they moved into the outlying districts of the city (where they replaced those now-affluent Americans of European stock who had moved out of the city entirely, to private homes in the suburbs). Some remained behind in the old neighborhood, succumbing to the deadly grinding jaws of poverty, and wondering occasionally what it had been like to swim in clear warm waters where the only possible threat was a barracuda.

The long-haired youths must have seemed like invading immigrants to the Puerto Ricans who still inhabited the area. It is easy to turn prejudice inside out; within every fat oppressor, there lurks a skinny victim waiting to be released. The hippies, the flower children, the "freaks" if you prefer, came seeking peace and talking love, and were greeted with the same fear, suspicion, hostility, and prejudice that had greeted the Puerto Ricans upon their arrival. In this case, however, it was the Puerto Ricans themselves who were doing the hating—you cannot teach people a way of life, and then expect them to put it conveniently aside. You cannot force them into a sewer and then expect them to understand why the sons and daughters of *successful* Americans are voluntarily seeking residence in that very same sewer. If violence of any kind is absurd, then victims attacking other victims is surely ludicrous. Such was the situation in the South Quarter, where the young people who had come there to do their thing had taken instead to buying pistols for protection against other people who had been trying to do *their* thing for more years than they could count. In recent months, bikies had begun drifting into the area, sporting their leather jackets and their swastikas and lavishing on their motorcycles the kind of love usually reserved for women. The bikies were bad news. Their presence added a tense note of uneasiness and unpredictability to an already volatile situation.

The Puerto Ricans Carella spoke to that afternoon did not enjoy talking to a cop. Cops meant false arrests, cops meant bribes, cops meant harassment. It occurred to him that Alex Delgado, the one Puerto Rican detective on the squad (in itself a comment) might have handled the investigation better, but he was stuck with it, and so he plunged ahead, showing the picture, asking the questions, getting the same response each time: *No, I do not know him. They all look alike to me.*

The bikie's name was Yank, meticulously lettered in white paint on the front of his leather jacket, over the heart. He had long frizzy black hair and a dense black beard. His eyes were blue, the right one partially closed by a scar that ran from his forehead to his cheek, crossing a portion of the lid in passing. He wore the usual gear in addition to the black leather jacket: the crushed peaked cap (his crash helmet was on the seat of his bike, parked at the curb), a black T-shirt (streaked white here and there from bleach-washing), black denim trousers, brass-studded big-buckled belt, black boots. An assortment of chains hung around his neck and the German iron cross dangled from one of them. He was sitting on a tilted wooden chair outside a shop selling posters (LBJ on a motorcycle in the window behind him), smoking a cigar and admiring the sleek chrome sculpture of his own bike at the curb. He did not even look at Carella as he approached. He knew instantly that Carella was a cop, but bikies don't know from cops. Bikies, in fact, sometimes think they themselves are the cops, and the bad guys are everybody else in the world.

Carella didn't waste time. He showed his shield and his I.D. card, and said, "Detective Carella, 87th Squad."

Yank regarded him with cool disdain, and then puffed on his cigar. "Yeah?" he said.

"We're trying to get a positive identification on a young man who may have been living in the neighborhood . . ."

"Yeah?"

"I thought you might be able to help."

"Why?"

"Do you live around here?"

"Yeah."

"How long have you been living here?"

"Three of us blew in from the Coast a few weeks back."

"Transients, huh?"

"Mobile, you might say."

"Where are you living?"

"Here and there."

"Where's that?"

"We drop in various places. Our club members are usually welcome everywhere."

"Where are you dropping in right now?"

"Around the corner."

"Around the corner where?"

"On Rutland. Listen, I thought you were trying to identify somebody. What're all these questions about? You charging me with some terrible crime?"

"Have you got a terrible crime in mind?"

"The bike's legally parked, I was sitting here smoking a cigar and meditating. Is that against the law?"

"Nobody said it was."

"So why all the questions?"

Carella reached into his jacket pocket, took out his notebook, and removed from it the photograph of the dead man. "Recognize him?" he asked, and handed the picture to Yank, who blew out a cloud of smoke, righted his chair, and then held the picture between his knees, hunched over it, as he studied it.

"Never saw him in my life," he said. He handed the picture back to Carella, tilted the chair against the wall again, and drew in another lungful of cigar smoke.

"I wonder if I could have your full name," Carella said.

"What for?"

"In case I need to get in touch with you again."

"Why would you need to get in touch with me? I just told you I never saw this guy in my life."

"Yes, but people sometimes come up with information later on. Since you and your friends are so mobile, you might just hear something that . . ."

"Tell you what," Yank said, and grinned. "You give me *your* name. If I hear anything, *I'll* call *you*." He blew two precise smoke rings into the air, and said, "How's that?"

"I've already given you my name," Carella said.

"Shows what kind of memory I've got," Yank said, and again grinned.

"I'll see you around," Carella said.

"Don't count on it," Yank answered.

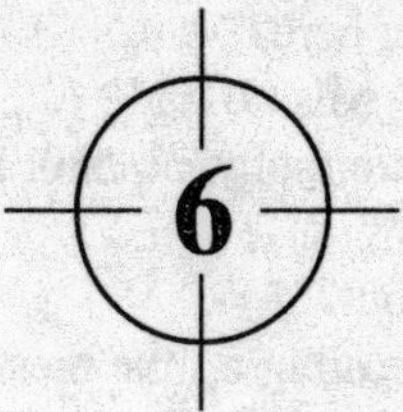

At ten minutes to one on Wednesday afternoon, Augusta Blair called the squadroom and asked to talk to Detective Kling, who was on his lunch hour and down the hall in the locker room, taking a nap. Meyer asked if Kling could call her back and she breathlessly told him she had only a minute and would appreciate it if he could be called to the phone. It had to do with the burglary, she said. Meyer went down the hall and reluctantly awakened Kling, who did not seem to mind at all. In fact, he hurried to his desk, picked up the receiver, and said, quite cheerfully, "Hello, Miss Blair, how are you?"

"Fine, thank you," she said. "I've been trying to call you all day long, Mr. Kling, but this is the first break we've had. We started at nine this morning, and I didn't know if you got to work that early."

"Yes, I was here," Kling said.

"I guess I should have called then. Anyway, here I am

now. And I've got to be back in a minute. Do you think you can come down here?"

"Where are you, Miss Blair?"

"Schaeffer Photography at 580 Hall Avenue. The fifth floor."

"What's this about?"

"When I was cleaning up the mess in the apartment, I found something that wasn't mine. I figure the burglar may have dropped it."

"I'll be right there," Kling said. "What was it you found?"

"Well, I'll show you when you get here," she said. "I've got to run, Mr. Kling."

"Okay," he said, "I'll . . ."

But she was gone.

Schaeffer Photography occupied the entire fifth floor of 580 Hall. The receptionist, a pert blonde with a marked German accent, informed Kling that Augusta had said he would be coming, and then directed him to the studio, which was at the end of a long hallway hung with samples of Schaeffer's work. Judging from the selection, Schaeffer did mostly fashion photography; no avid reader of Vogue, Kling nonetheless recognized the faces of half the models, and searched in vain for a picture of Augusta. Apparently she had been telling the truth when she said she'd been in the business only a short while.

The door to the studio was closed. Kling eased it open, and found himself in an enormous room overhung by a skylight. A platform was at the far end of the room, the wall behind it hung with red backing paper. Four power packs rested on the floor, with cables running to strobe lights on stands, their gray, umbrella-shaped reflectors angled toward the platform. Redheaded Augusta Blair, wearing a red blouse, a short red jumper, red knee socks, and red patent leather pumps, stood before the red backing paper. A young girl in jeans and a Snoopy sweatshirt stood to the right of the platform, her arms folded across her chest. The photographer and his assistant were hunched over a tripod-mounted Polaroid. They took several pictures, strobe lights flashing for a fraction of a second each time they pressed the shutter release, and then, apparently satisfied with the exposure setting, removed the Polaroid from its mount and replaced it with a Nikon. Augusta spotted Kling standing near the door, grinned, and waggled the fingers of her right hand at him. The photographer turned.

"Yes?" he said.

"He's a friend of mine," Augusta said.

"Oh, okay," the photographer said in dismissal. "Make yourself comfortable, keep it quiet. You ready, honey? Where's David?"

"David!" the assistant called, and a man rushed over from where he'd been standing at a wall phone, partially hidden by a screen over which was draped a pair of purple pantyhose. He went directly to Augusta, combed her hair swiftly, and then stepped off the platform.

"Okay?" the photographer asked.

"Ready," Augusta said.

"The headline is 'Red On Red,' God help us, and the idea—"

"What's the matter with the headline?" the girl in the Snoopy sweatshirt asked.

"Nothing, Helen, far be it from me to cast aspersions on your magazine. Gussie, the idea is to get this big *red* feeling, you know what I mean? Everything bursting and screaming and, you know, *red* as hell, okay? You know what I want?"

"I think so," Augusta said.

"We want *red*," Helen said.

"What the hell's this proxar doing on here?" the photographer asked.

"I thought we'd be doing close stuff," his assistant said.

"No, Eddie, get it off here, will you?"

"Sure," Eddie said, and began unscrewing the lens.

"David, get that hair off her forehead, will you?"

"Where?"

"Right there, hanging over her eye, don't you see it there?"

"Oh yeah."

"Yeah, that's it, thank you. Eddie, how we doing?"

"You've got it."

"Gussie?"

"Yep."

"Okay then, here we go, now give me that big *red,* Gussie, that's what I want, I want this thing to yell *red* all over town, that's the girl, more of that, now tilt the head, that's good, Gussie, smile now, more teeth, honey, red, *red,* throw your arms wide, good, good, that's it, now you're beginning to feel it, let it bubble up, honey, let it burst out of your fingertips, nice, I like that, give me that with a, that's it, good, now the other side, the head the other way, no, no, keep the arms out, fine, that's good, all right now come toward me, no, honey, don't slink, this isn't blue, it's *red,* you've got to *explode* toward, *yes,* that's it, yes, *yes,* good, now with more *hip,* Gussie, fine, I like that, I like it, eyes wider, toss the hair, good, honey . . ."

For the next half hour Kling watch as Augusta exhibited to the camera a wide variety of facial expressions, body positions, and acrobatic contortions, looking nothing less than beautiful in every pose she struck. The only sounds in the huge room were the photographer's voice and the clicking of his camera. Coaxing, scolding, persuading, approving, suggesting, chiding, cajoling, the voice went on and on, barely audible except to Augusta, while the tiny clicking of the camera accompanied the running patter like a soft-shoe routine. Kling was fascinated. In Augusta's apartment the other night, he had been overwhelmed by her beauty, but had not suspected her vitality. Reacting to the burglary, she had presented a solemn, dispirited façade, so that her beauty seemed unmarred but essentially lifeless. Now, as Kling watched her bursting with energy and ideas to convey the concept of red, the camera clicking, the photographer circling her and talking to her, she seemed another person entirely, and he wondered suddenly how many faces Augusta Blair owned, and how many of them he would get to know.

"Okay, great, Gussie," the photographer said, "let's break for ten minutes. Then we'll do those sailing outfits, Helen. Eddie, can we get some coffee?"

"Right away."

Augusta came down off the platform and walked to where Kling was standing at the back of the room. "Hi," she said. "I'm sorry I kept you waiting."

"I enjoyed it," Kling said.

"It *was* kind of fun," Augusta said. "Most of them aren't."

"Which of these do you want her in first, Helen?" the photographer asked.

"The one with the striped top."

"You *do* want me to shoot both of them, right?"

"Yes. The two *tops*. There's only one pair of pants," Helen said.

"Okay, both tops, the striped one first. You going to introduce me to your friend, Gussie?" he said, and walked to where Kling and Augusta were standing.

"Rick Schaeffer," she said, "this is Detective Kling. I'm sorry, I don't know your first name."

"Bert," he said.

"Nice to meet you," Schaeffer said, and extended his hand. The men shook hands briefly, and Schaeffer said, "Is this about the burglary?"

"Yes," Kling said.

"Well, look, I won't take up your time," Schaeffer said. "Gussie, honey, we'll be shooting the striped top first."

"Okay."

"I want to go as soon as we change the no-seam."

"I'll be ready."

"Right. Nice meeting you, Bert."

He walked off briskly toward where two men were carrying a roll of blue backing paper to the platform.

"What did you find in the apartment?" Kling asked.

"I've got it in my bag," Augusta said. She began walking toward a bench on the side of the room, Kling following. "Listen, I must apologize for the rush act, but they're paying me twenty-five dollars an hour, and they don't like me sitting around."

"I understand," Kling said.

Augusta dug into her bag and pulled out a ballpoint pen, which she handed to Kling and which, despite the fact that her fingerprints were already all over it, he accepted on a tented handkerchief. The top half of the pen was made of metal, brass-plated to resemble gold. The bottom half of the pen was made of black plastic. The pen was obviously a give-away item. Stamped onto the plastic in white letters were the words:

Sulzbacher Realty
1142 Ashmead Avenue
Calm's Point

"You're sure it isn't yours?" Kling asked.

"Positive. Will it help you?"

"It's a start."

"Good." She glanced over her shoulder toward where the men were rolling down the blue seamless. "What time is it, Bert?"

Kling looked at his watch. "Almost two. What do I call you? Augusta or Gussie?"

"Depends on what we're doing," she said, and smiled.

"What are we doing tonight?" Kling asked immediately.

"I'm busy," Augusta said.

"How about tomorrow?"

She looked at him for a moment, seemed to make a swift decision, and then said, "Let me check my book." She reached into her bag for an appointment calendar, opened it, said, "What's tomorrow, Thursday?" and without waiting for his answer, flipped open to the page marked Thursday, April 22. "No, not tomorrow, either," she said, and Kling figured he had got the message loud and clear. "I'm free Saturday night, though," she said, surprising him. "How's Saturday?"

"Saturday's fine," he said quickly. "Dinner?"

"I'd love to."

"And maybe a movie later."

"Why don't we do it the other way around? If you won't mind how I look, you can pick me up at the studio . . ."

"Fine . . ."

"Around six, six-fifteen, and we can catch an early movie, and then maybe grab a hamburger or something later on. What time do you quit work?"

"I'll certainly be free by six."

"Okay, the photographer's name is Jerry Bloom, and he's at 1204 Concord. The second floor, I think. Aren't you going to write it down?"

"Jerry Bloom," Kling said, "1204 Concord, the second floor, at six o'clock."

"Gussie, let's go!" Schaeffer shouted.

"Saturday," she said and, to Kling's vast amazement, touched her fingers to her lips, blew him an unmistakable kiss, grinned, and walked swiftly to where Rick Schaeffer was waiting.

Kling blinked.

Ashmead Avenue was in the shadow of the elevated structure in downtown Calm's Point, not far from the bustling business section and the Academy of Music. When Kling was seventeen years old he had dated a girl from Calm's Point, and had sworn never again. The date had been for eight-thirty, and he had left Riverhead at seven sharp, taking the train on Allen and riding for an hour and a half before getting off at Kingston Parkway as she had instructed him. He had then proceeded to lose himself in the labyrinthine streets with their alien names, arriving at her house at 10 P.M., to be told by her mother that she had gone to a movie with a girlfriend. He had asked if he should wait, and the girl's mother had looked at him as though he were retarded and had said simply, "I would not suggest it." Rarely did he come to Calm's Point anymore, unless he was called there on an investigation.

Sulzbacher Realty was in a two-story brick building sandwiched between a supermarket and a liquor store. The entrance door was between two plate-glass windows adorned with photographs of houses in and around the area. Through the glass Kling could see a pair of desks. A man sat at one of them studying an open book before him. He looked up as Kling came into the office.

"Good afternoon," he said, "may I help you?"

He was wearing a brown business suit, a white shirt, and a striped tie. A local Chamber of Commerce pin was in his lapel, and the tops of several cigars protruded from the breast pocket of his jacket.

"I hope so," Kling said. He took out his wallet, and opened it. "I'm Detective Kling," he said, "87th Squad. I'd like to ask you some questions."

"Have a seat," the man answered, and indicated the wooden chair alongside his desk. "I'm Fred Lipton, be happy to help you any way I can."

"Mr. Lipton, one of your company pens was found at the scene of a burglary, and we . . ."

"Company pens?"

"Yes, sir. The name of the company lettered on the barrel."

"Oh, yes. *Those.* The ones Nat bought to advertise the business."

"Nat?"

"Nat Sulzbacher. He owns the company. I'm just a salesman." Lipton opened the top drawer of his desk, reached into it, opened his hand, and dropped a half dozen ballpoint pens onto the desk top. "Are these the ones you mean?"

Kling picked one up and looked at it. "Yes," he said, "a pen similar to these."

The front door opened, and a tall, dark-haired man entered the room. "Afternoon, Fred," he said. "Selling lots of houses?"

"Mr. Sulzbacher, this is Detective . . ."

"Kling."

"Kling. He's investigating a burglary."

"Yeah?" Sulzbacher said, and raised his eyebrows in appreciation.

"They found one of our pens at the scene of the crime."

"One of ours?" Sulzbacher said. "May I see it, please?"

"I don't have it with me right now."

"Then how do I know it's ours?"

"Our name's on it," Lipton said.

"Oh. So what would you like to know, young man?"

"Since the pen was found at the scene of a crime . . ."

"You don't think we're criminals here, do you?"

"No. I was merely wondering . . ."

"Because if that's what you think, you're mistaken. We're real estate agents here. *That's* what we are."

"No one's suggesting you or Mr. Lipton burglarized an apartment. All I wanted to know is whether you give these pens to anybody special, or whether . . ."

"You know how many of these pens I ordered?" Sulzbacher asked.

"How many?"

"Five thousand."

"Oh," Kling said.

"You know how many of them we've given out in the past six months? At least half that amount. Certainly two thousand, anyway. So you expect us to remember who we gave them to?"

"Were these customers or . . . ?"

"Customers, sure, but also strangers. Somebody comes in, asks about a house, we give him a little pen so he won't forget the name. There are a lot of real estate agents in Calm's Point, you know."

"Mmm," Kling said.

"I'm sorry," Sulzbacher said.

"Yeah," Kling said. "Me too."

This time, they did not think it was a mistake.

The duplicate photostat arrived in the afternoon mail, and was promptly added to the gallery on the bulletin board, so that the squad now proudly possessed two pictures of J. Edgar Hoover and two pictures of George Washington.

"What do you think he's driving at?" Hawes asked.

"I don't know," Carella said.

"It's deliberate, that's for sure," Meyer said.

"No question."

The three men stood before the bulletin board, hands on hips, studying the photostats as though they were hanging on the wall of a museum.

"Where do you suppose he got the pictures?" Hawes asked.

"Newspapers, I would guess. Books. Magazines."

"Any help for us there?"

"I doubt it. Even if we located the source, what good . . . ?"

"Yeah."

"The important thing is what he's trying to tell us."

"What do we know so far?" Meyer asked.

"So far we know he's going to steal half a million dollars on April thirtieth," Hawes said.

"No, that's not it exactly," Carella said.

"What is it exactly?"

"He said, 'With your assistance . . .' remember? 'With your *assistance,* I'm going to steal five hundred thousand dollars on the last day of April.'"

"*Whose* assistance?" Meyer asked.

"Ours, I guess," Carella said.

"Or maybe yours *personally,*" Hawes said. "You're the one he was talking to."

"That's right, yeah," Carella said.

"And the pictures have all been addressed to you."

"Yeah."

"Maybe he figures you've got something in common. Maybe all this crap is pegged directly at you."

"We *have* got something in common," Carella said.

"What's that?"

"We shot each other. And survived."

"So what do you think?" Hawes said.

"What do you mean?"

"If he's pegging it at you, what do you think? Have you got any ideas?"

"Not a single one," Carella said.

"Hoover and Washington," Meyer said thoughtfully. "What have *they* got in common?"

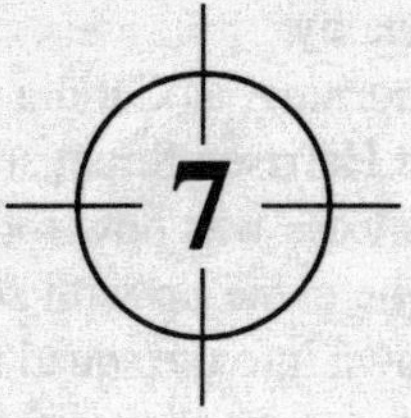

"The Jesus Case," as it was playfully dubbed by the heathens of the 87th Squad, was going nowhere very quickly. The dead man had still not been identified, and Carella knew that, unless a positive identification was made within the next few days, the case was in danger of being buried as deep as the corpse had been. Until they knew who he was, until they could say with certainty that *this* man with *this* name was slain by person or persons unknown, why then he would remain only what Dr. Cortez had labeled him last Monday: a corpse. Labels. A corpse. Anonymous. A lifeless heap of human rubble, unmissed, unreported, unidentified when it was buried in the municipal cemetery. There were too many murder victims in the city, all of them with names and addresses and relatives and histories. It was too much to ask of any overworked police department that it should spend valuable time trying to find the murderer of someone who had namelessly roamed the streets. A cipher never evokes much sympathy.

On Thursday morning, as Carella made his way from shop to shop in the Harrison Street area, it began raining heavily. The Jesus Case was now four days old. Carella knew that, unless he came up with something soon, the case would be thrown into the squad's Open File. For all intents and purposes, such disposition would mean that the case was closed. Not solved, merely closed until something accidentally turned up on it weeks or months or years later, if ever. The idea of burying the case a scant two days after the body itself had been buried was extremely distasteful to Carella. Aside from his revulsion for the brutality of the crucifixion (if such it could be called; there had, after all, been no cross involved), Carella suspected that something deeper within him was being touched. He had not been inside a church since the day his sister got married, more than thirteen years ago, but he felt vague stirrings now, memories of priests with thuribles, the heavy musk of incense, altar boys in white, the crucified form of Jesus Christ high above the altar. He had not been a religious child, nor was he a religious man. But the murdered man was curiously linked in his mind to the spiritual concept of someone dying for humanity, and he could not accept the idea that the man in the abandoned tenement had died for nothing at all.

The rain swept the pavements like machine-gun fire in some gray disputed no-man's land. A jagged lance of lightning crackled across the sky, followed by a boom of thunder that rattled Carella to his shoelaces. He ran for the nearest shop, threw open the door, shook water from his trench coat, and mopped his head with a handkerchief. Only then did he look around him. He first thought he was in an art gallery having a one-man show. He then realized he was in a sculptor's shop, the artist's work displayed on long tables and shelves, female nudes of various sizes sculpted in wood and stone, cast in plaster and bronze. The work was quite good, or at least it seemed so to Carella. Naturalistic, almost photographic, the nudes sat or stood or lay on their sides in frozen three-dimensional realism, some of them no larger than a fist, others standing some three or four feet tall. The artist had used the same model for all of the pieces, an obviously young girl, tall and slender, with small well-formed breasts and narrow hips, long hair trailing halfway down her back. The effect was of being in a mirrored room that reflected the same girl in a dozen different poses, shrinking her to less than human size and capturing her life force in materials firmer than flesh. Carella was studying one of the statues more closely when a man came out of the back room.

The man was in his late twenties, a tall blond man with dark brown eyes and a leonine head. He was on crutches. His left leg was heavily bandaged. A tattered white tennis sneaker was on his right foot.

There were, Carella surmised, possibly ten thousand men in this city at this moment who were wearing white tennis sneakers on their right feet, their left feet, and perhaps even *both* feet. He did not know how many of them had a shop on King's Circle, though, four blocks from Harrison Street, where a boy had been nailed to the wall five days ago, and where a left-footed tennis sneaker had been found in an empty apartment down the hall.

"Yes, sir?" the man said. "May I help you?"

"I'm a police officer," Carella said.

"Uh-huh," the man said.

"Detective Carella, 87th Squad."

"Uh-huh," he said again. He did not ask for identification, and Carella did not show any.

"I'm investigating a homicide," he said.

"I see." The man nodded, and then hobbled on his crutches to one of the long tables. He sat on the edge of it, beside a sculpture of his slender young model at repose in bronze, legs crossed, head bent, eyes downcast like a naked nun. "My name's Sanford Elliot," he said. "Sandy, everybody calls me. Who was killed?"

"We don't know. That's why I've been going around the neighborhood."

"When did it happen?" Elliot asked.

"Last Sunday night."

"I was out of town last Sunday," Elliot said, and Carella suddenly wondered why he felt compelled to establish an alibi for a murder that had thus far been discussed only in the most ambiguous terms.

"Really?" Carella said. "Where were you?"

"Boston. I went up to Boston for the weekend."

"Nice up there," Carella said.

"Yes."

"Anyway, I've been showing a picture of the victim..."

"I don't know too many people in the neighborhood," Elliot said. "I've only been here in the city since January. I keep mostly to myself. Do my work in the studio back there, and try to sell it out front here. I don't know too many people."

"Well, lots of people come in and out of the shop, don't they?" Carella said.

"Oh, sure. But unless they buy one of my pieces, I never get to know their names. You see what I mean?"

"Sure," Carella said. "Why don't you take a look at the picture, anyway?"

"Well, if you like. It won't do any good, though. I really don't know too many people around here."

"Are you from Boston originally?"

"What?"

"You said you went up to Boston, I figured . . ."

"Oh. No, I'm from Oregon. But I went to art school up there. School of Fine Arts at B.U. Boston University."

"And you say you were up there Sunday?"

"That's right. I went up to see some friends. I've got a lot of friends in the Boston area."

"But not too many around here."

"No, not around here."

"Did you hurt your leg before you went to Boston, or after you came back?"

"Before."

"Went up there on crutches, huh?"

"Yes."

"Did you drive up?"

"A friend drove me."

"Who?"

"The girl who poses for me." He made a vague gesture at the pieces of sculpture surrounding them.

"What's wrong with the leg, anyway?" Carella asked.

"I had an accident."

"Is it broken?"

"No. I sprained the ankle."

"Those can be worse than a break, sometimes."

"Yeah, that's what the doctor said."

"Who's the doctor?"

"Why do you want to know?"

"Just curious."

"Well," Elliot said, "I don't think that's any of your business."

"You're right," Carella said, "it isn't. Would you mind looking at this picture?"

"I mean," Elliot said, gathering steam, "I've given you a lot of time as it is. I was working when you came in. I don't like being disturbed when I'm . . ."

"I'm sorry," Carella said. "If you'll just look at this picture . . ."

"I won't know who he is, anyway," Elliot said. "I hardly know any of the guys in this neighborhood. Most of my friends are up in Boston."

"Well, take a look," Carella said, and handed him the photograph.

"No, I don't know him," Elliot said, and handed it back almost at once.

Carella put the photograph into his notebook, turned up the collar of his coat, said, "Thanks," and went out into the rain. It was coming down in buckets; he was willing to forsake the goddamn May flowers. He began running the instant he hit the street, and did not stop until he reached the open diner on the corner. Inside, he expelled his breath in the exaggerated manner of all people who have run through rain and finally reached shelter, took off his trench coat, hung it up, and sat at the counter. A waitress slouched over and asked him what he wanted. He ordered a cup of coffee and a cheese Danish.

There was a lot that bothered him about Sanford Elliot.

He was bothered by the tattered white tennis sneaker, and he was bothered by the fact that Elliot's *left* foot was in bandages—or was it only coincidence that the sneaker they'd found was left-footed? He was bothered by the speedy alibi Elliot had offered for his whereabouts on the night of the murder, and bothered by the thought of a man on crutches taking a long car trip up to Boston, even if he was being driven by someone.

Why hadn't Elliot been willing to tell him the name of his doctor? And how had Elliot known that the murder victim was a man? Even before Carella showed him the photograph, he had said, "I won't know who he is, anyway." *He.* When up to that time Carella had spoken of the dead man only as "the victim."

Something else was bothering him.

The waitress put his cup of coffee on the counter, sloshing it into the saucer. He picked up his Danish, bit into it, put it down, lifted the coffee cup, slipped a paper napkin between cup and saucer, drank some coffee, and suddenly knew what was nudging his memory.

He debated going back to the shop.

Elliot had mentioned that he'd been working when Carella came in; the possibility existed that the girl was still with him. He decided instead to wait a while and talk to her alone, without Elliot there to prompt her.

He finished his coffee and Danish, called the squadroom to find out if there had been any messages, and was informed by Meyer that another manila envelope had arrived in the mail. Carella asked him to open it. When Meyer got back on the line, he said, "Well, what is it this time?"

"An airplane," Meyer said.

"A what?"

"A picture of an airplane."

"What kind of an airplane?"

"Beats the hell out of me," Meyer said.

It was Cotton Hawes who positively identified the airplane.

"That's a Zero," he said, looking at the photostat now pinned to the bulletin board at the end of the row that contained two pictures of J. Edgar Hoover and two pictures of George Washington. Hawes had been Chief Torpedoman aboard a PT boat throughout the war in the Pacific and presumably knew whereof he spoke; Meyer accepted his word without hesitation.

"But why?" he said.

"Who the hell knows? How does a picture of a Japanese fighter plane tie in with Hoover and Washington?"

"Maybe the Japanese are planning an attack on the FBI in Washington," Meyer said.

"Right," Hawes said. "Six squadrons of Zekes zooming in low over Pennsylvania Avenue."

"Pearl Harbor all over again."

"Beginning of World War III."

"Must be that," Meyer said. "What else could it be?"

"And the Deaf Man, realizing we're the nation's only hope, is warning us and hoping we'll sound the clarion."

"Go sound the clarion, Cotton."

"You know what I think?" Hawes said.

"Tell me, pray."

"I think this time he's putting us on. I don't think there's any connection at all between those stats."

"Then why send them to us?"

"Because he's a pain in the ass, plain and simple. He snips unrelated pictures out of newspapers, magazines, and books, has them photostated, and then mails them to us, hoping they'll drive us crazy."

"What about the threat he made?"

"What about it? Carella's going to help him steal half a million bucks, huh? Fat chance of that happening."

"Cotton?" Meyer said.

"Mmm?"

"If this was anybody else we were dealing with here, I would say, 'Yes, you're right, he's a bedbug.' But this is the Deaf Man. When the Deaf Man says he is going to do something, he does it. I don't know what connection there is between those stats, but I know there is a connection, and I know he's hoping we're smart enough to figure it out."

"Why?" Hawes said.

"Because once we figure it out, he'll do something related but unrelated. Cotton . . ."

"Yes, Meyer?"

"Cotton," Meyer said, and looked up seriously, and

said with great intensity, "Cotton, this man is a diabolical *fiend!*"

"Steady now," Hawes said.

"Cotton, I detest this man. Cotton, I wish I had never heard of this villain in my entire life."

"Try to get hold of yourself," Hawes said.

"How can we *possibly* figure out the associations his maniacal mind has concocted?"

"Look, Meyer, you're letting this . . ."

"How can we *possibly* know what these images mean to him? Hoover, Washington, and a goddamn Jap Zero!" Meyer stabbed his finger at the photostat of the airplane. "Maybe that's *all* he's trying to tell us, Cotton."

"What do you mean?"

"That so far we've got nothing. Zero. A big fat empty circle. Zero, zero, zero."

"Would you like a cup of coffee?" Hawes asked kindly.

Carella hit four apartment buildings on Porter Street before he found a mailbox listing for Henry Scaffale. He climbed the steps to the third floor, listened outside Apartment 32, heard voices inside but could not distinguish what they were saying. He knocked on the door.

"Who is it?" a man's voice asked.

"Me," Carella said. "Detective Carella."

There was a short silence. Carella waited. He heard someone approaching the door. It opened a crack, and Bob Carmody looked out.

"Yes?" he said. "What do you want?"

"Mary Margaret here?"

"Maybe."

"I'd like to talk to her."

"What about?"

"Is she here?"

"Maybe you'd better come back with a warrant," Bob said, and began closing the door.

Carella immediately wedged his foot into it, and said, "I can do that, Bob, but going all the way downtown isn't going to sweeten my disposition by the time I get back. What do you say?"

"Let him in, Bob," a girl's voice said.

Bob scowled, opened the door, and stepped aside to let Carella in. Mary Margaret was sitting on a mattress on the floor. A chubby girl wearing a pink sweater and jeans was sitting beside her. Both girls had their backs to the wall. Hank was straddling a kitchen chair, his chin on his folded arms, watching Carella as he came into the room.

"Hello, Mary Margaret," Carella said.

"Hello," she answered without enthusiasm.

"I'd like to talk to you."

"Talk," she said.

"Privately."

"Where would you suggest? There's only this one room and a john."

"How about the hallway?"

Mary Margaret shrugged, shoved her long hair back over her shoulders with both hands, rose with a dancer's motion from her cross-legged position, and walked barefooted past Carella and into the hallway. Carella followed her out and closed the door behind them.

"What do you want to talk about?" she asked.

"Do you pose for an artist named Sandy Elliot?"

"Why?" Mary Margaret asked. "Is that against the law? I'm nineteen years old."

"No, it's not against the law."

"So, okay, I pose for him. How'd *you* know that?"

"I saw some of his work. The likeness is remarkable." Carella paused. "Do you also *drive* for him?"

"What are you talking about?"

"Did you drive him up to Boston last weekend?"

"Yes," Mary Margaret said.

"Were you posing for him today when I went to the shop?"

"I don't know when you went to the shop."

"Let's take just the first part. Were you posing for him today?"

"Yes."

"What time?"

"From ten o'clock on."

"I was there about eleven."

"I didn't know that."

"Sandy didn't mention my visit?"

"No."

"When did he hurt his leg, Mary Margaret?"

"I don't know."

"When was the last time you posed for him?"

"Before today, do you mean?"

"Yes."

"Last Thursday."

Carella took a small celluloid calendar from his wallet and looked at it. "That would be Thursday, the fifteenth."

"Yes, I guess so."

"Was he on crutches at that time?"

"Yes."

"When did you pose for him before that?"

"I pose for him every Thursday morning."

"Does that mean you posed for him on Thursday, April eighth?"

"Yes."

"Was he on crutches then?"

"No."

"So he hurt himself sometime between the eighth and the fifteenth, is that right?"

"I guess so. What difference does it make *when* he . . . ?"

"Where'd you go in Boston?"

"Oh, around."

"Around where?"

"I don't know Boston too well. Sandy was giving me directions."

"When did you leave here?"

"Friday."

"Friday, the sixteenth?"

"Mmm."

"Was it?"

"Yes, it was. Last Friday. Right."

"What kind of car did you use?"

"Sandy's."

"Which is what?"

"Little Volkswagen."

"Must have been uncomfortable. Crutches and all."

"Mmm."

"How long did it take you to get up there?"

"Oh, I don't know. Four, five hours. Something like that."

"What time did you leave?"

"Here? The city?"

"Yes."

"In the morning."

"What time in the morning?"

"Nine? Ten? I don't remember."

"Did you come back down that night?"

"No. We stayed a few days. In Boston."

"Where?"

"One of Sandy's friends."

"And came back when?"

"Late Monday night."

"And today you posed for Sandy again."

"That's right."

"How much does he pay you?"

Mary Margaret hesitated.

"How much does he pay you?" Carella asked again.

"Sandy's my boyfriend," she said. "He doesn't pay me anything."

"Where do you pose?"

"In the back of his shop. He's got his studio there. In the back."

"Are you living with him, Mary Margaret?"

"I live here. But I spend most of my time with Sandy."

"Would you know the name of the doctor who treated his foot?"

"No."

"What happened to it, anyway?"

"He had an accident."

"Fell, did he?"

"Yes."

"And tore the Achilles tendon, huh?"

"Yes."

"Mary Margaret, do you think Sandy might have known that man in the picture I showed you?"

"Go ask Sandy."

"I did."

"So what did he say?"

"He said no."

"Then I guess he didn't know him."

"Did you know him?"

"No."

"You want to know what I think, Mary Margaret?"

"What?"

"I think Sandy was lying."

Mary Margaret shrugged.

"I think you're lying, too."

"Why would I lie?"

"I don't know yet," Carella said.

He had been inside the apartment for perhaps twenty minutes when he heard a key turning in the lock. He knew that the Ungermans would be gone until the end of the week, and at first he thought the building superintendent was making an inopportune, routine check, but then he heard a man say, "Good to be home, eh, Karin?" and realized the Ungermans were back, and he was in the bedroom, and there were no exterior fire escapes; the only way out was through the front door, the way he had come in. He decided immediately that there was no percentage in waiting, the thing to do was make his move at once. The Ungermans were a couple in their late sixties, he would have no trouble getting past them, the difficult thing would be getting out of the building. They were moving toward the bedroom, Harry Ungerman carrying a pair of suitcases, his wife a step behind him, reaching up to take off her hat, when he charged them. He knocked Ungerman flat on his back, and then shoved out at Mrs. Ungerman, who reached out toward him for support, clutching at his clothes to keep from falling over backward the way her husband had done not ten seconds before. They danced an awkward, silent little jig for perhaps four seconds, her hands grasping, he trying to shove her away, and finally he wrenched loose, slamming her against the wall, and racing for the front door. He got the door unlocked, opened it, and was running for the stairway at the far end of the hall when Mrs. Ungerman began screaming.

Instead of heading down for the street, he went up toward the roof of the twelve-story building. The metal door was locked when he reached it. He backed off several paces, sprang the lock with a flat-footed kick, and sprinted out onto the roof. He hesitated a moment in the star-drenched night, to get his bearings. Then he ran for the parapet, looked down at the roof of the adjacent building, and leaped.

By the time Harry Ungerman put in his call to the police, the man who had tried to burglarize his apartment was already four blocks away, entering his own automobile.

But it had been a close call.

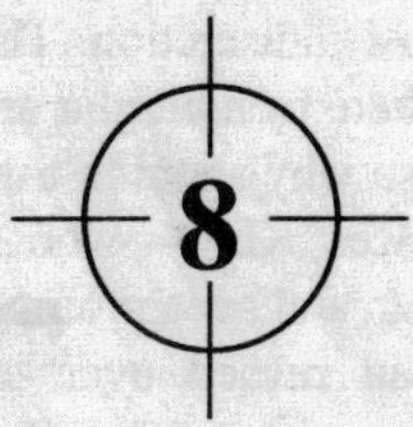

If you are going to go tiptoeing into empty apartments, you had best make certain they are going to *stay* empty all the while you are illegally on the premises. If they suddenly become anything less than empty, it is best not to try pushing around an elderly lady with a bad back, since she just might possibly grab you to keep from falling on her coccyx, and in the ensuing gavotte might get a very good look at you, particularly if she is a sharp-eyed old bat.

Karin Ungerman was a very sharp-eyed old bat, and mad as a hornet besides. What annoyed her particularly was the kitten. The kitten was a fluffy little tan thing who had wet on the gold brocade chaise in the Ungerman bedroom. Mrs. Ungerman was certain the stain would not come out, despite liberal and repeated sprinklings of a highly touted spot remover. The first thing she asked Kling when he arrived that morning was whether or not her insurance company would pay damages for the kitten's indiscretion. The kitten had, after all, been brought there by a burglar and she was covered for fire and theft, so why shouldn't they pay? Kling did not know the answer. Kling—who had arrived at the squadroom at 8 A.M., and been promptly informed of last night's events—had rushed over to 641 Richardson Drive immediately, and was interested only in getting a description of the man both Ungermans had seen.

The Ungermans informed him that the only thing missing was a gold and pearl pin but that perhaps Karin Ungerman had given that to her sister who lived in Florida, she wasn't quite sure. The burglar had undoubtedly been in the apartment for only a very short while; only the top drawer of the dresser had been disturbed. Luckily, Mrs. Ungerman hid all her good jewelry in a galosh in the closet whenever she went on a trip. If you lived to be sixty-eight years old, and have been burglarized four times in the past seventeen years, you learn how to deal with the bastards. But bringing in a cat to pee all over your gold brocade chaise! Really!

"What did the man look like, can you tell me that?" Kling asked.

"He was a tall man," Mrs. Ungerman said.

"How tall?"

"Taller than you," she said.

"Six feet two inches, around there," Mr. Ungerman said.

"How was he dressed?"

"In dark clothes. Black, I think."

"Blue," Mr. Ungerman said.

"Dark, anyway," Mrs. Ungerman said. "Trousers, jacket, shirt, all dark."

"What kind of shirt?"

"A turtleneck," Mrs. Ungerman said.

"Was he a white man or a black man?"

"White. The part of his face we could see."

"What do you mean?"

"We only saw his eyes and forehead. He was wearing a mask."

"What kind of a mask?"

"A handkerchief. Over the bridge of his nose, hanging down over his face."

"You say you saw his eyes . . ."

"Yes, and his forehead."

"And his hair, too," Mr. Ungerman said. "He wasn't wearing a hat."

"What color were his eyes?" Kling asked.

"Brown."

"And his hair?"

"Black."

"Was it straight, wavy, curly?"

"Curly."

"Long or close-cropped?"

"Just average length," Mrs. Ungerman said.

"Anything else you may have noticed about him?"

"Nothing. Except that he moved very fast."

"I'd move fast, too," Mrs. Ungerman said, "if I'd just let a cat make a mess all over somebody's gold brocade chaise."

That morning Detective Steve Carella went down to the Criminal Courts Building and, being duly sworn, deposed and said in writing:

1. I am a detective in the Police Department assigned to the 87th Detective Squad.

2. I have information based upon my personal knowledge and belief and facts disclosed to me by the Medical Examiner that a murder has been committed. Investigation discloses the following:

On April 19th, at 10:15 A.M., George Mossler, a vagrant, discovered the body of an unidentified man in Apartment 51 of an abandoned tenement building at 433 North Harrison Street. The victim had been stabbed in the chest and nailed to the wall, a spike through each extended palm and a third spike through his crossed feet. Medical Examiner states cause of death to be cardiac hemorrhage due to penetrating knife wound; and sets time of death as sometime during the night of April 18th.

A search of the building at 433 North Harrison Street resulted in the finding of a size twelve, left-footed, white tennis sneaker in Apartment 52 which is down the hall from Apartment 51 where the body was discovered.

On April 22nd, while showing pictures of the body of the dead man to people in the neighborhood where the body was found, investigator entered the shop of Sanford Elliot, located at 1211 King's Circle, approximately four blocks from the North Harrison Street address. Sanford Elliot was on crutches and his left foot was bandaged. On his right foot was a white tennis sneaker believed to be the mate to the left-footed sneaker found at the murder scene. When questioned, Sanford Elliot stated that he had been in Boston on the night of April 18th and did not know or recognize the picture of the man found murdered at the North Harrison Street address.

Based upon the foregoing reliable information and upon my personal knowledge, there is probable cause to believe that aforementioned tennis sneaker constitutes evidence in the crime of murder and may be found in the possession of Sanford Elliot or at premises 1211 King's Circle, ground floor rear.

Wherefore, I respectfully request that the court issue a warrant and order of seizure, in the form annexed authorizing the search of Sanford Elliot and of premises 1211 King's Circle, ground floor rear, and directing that if such property or evidence or any part thereof be found that it be seized and brought before the court, together with such other and further relief that the court may deem proper.

No previous application in this matter has been made in this or any other court or to any other judge, justice, or magistrate.

Stephen Louis Carella 764-5632 Det/2nd 87th Squad

Police Officer Shield Rank Command

Carella realized that the application was weak in that there was no way of connecting Elliot with the murder except through the sneaker, and sneakers were, after all, fairly common wearing apparel. He knew, too, that a warrant issued on his application might possibly be later controverted on a motion to suppress the evidence seized under it. He was somewhat surprised, but nonetheless grateful, when a supreme court judge signed and dated the application, and issued the requested warrant.

Which meant that Carella now had the legal right to arrest an inanimate object, so to speak.

If Carella was getting a little help from the courts, Kling was simultaneously getting a little help from the Identification Section. As a matter of routine, he had asked them to run checks on both Fred Lipton and Nat Sulzbacher, the Calm's Point real estate agents whose giveaway pen had been found in Augusta Blair's apartment. Much to his surprise, the I.S. had come back with a positive identification that immediately catapulted old Fred Lipton into the role of prime suspect in the burglary case. Kling had not yet eliminated Stanislaw Janik as a contender for best supporting player and possible supplier of kittens and keys, but the physical description given by Mrs. Ungerman ruled him out as the man actually entering the apartments. The burglar was tall, with black curly hair and brown eyes. Janik was short, almost totally bald, and his blue eyes were magnified by thick eyeglasses.

So Kling was pleased to learn that whereas Nat Sulzbacher had no criminal record (he could have obtained a license to sell real estate after having been convicted of a misdemeanor), his salesman, Frederick Horace Lipton, had been in trouble with the law on two previous occasions, having been arrested for Disorderly Conduct back in 1954 and for First-Degree Forgery in 1957. The disturbance in 1954 was only a misdemeanor, defined as any crime other than a felony, but it still might have netted Lipton as much as six months' imprisonment in a county jail or workhouse. Instead, all he'd got was a $50 fine. The 1957 paper-hanging rap was a felony, of course, defined as a crime punishable by death or imprisonment in a state prison. Considering the offense, the court was equally charitable in sentencing Lipton this second time; he could have got twenty years, but he drew only ten.

He had served three and a half of those at Castleview State Prison, and had been released on parole in 1961. As far as society was concerned, he had paid his debt and was now a hard-working real estate salesman in Calm's Point. But one of his employer's give-away pens had been found at the scene of a burglary. Nat Sulzbacher did not have a criminal record; he was therefore an ordinary respectable everyday citizen. But Fred Lipton was an ex-con. So Kling naturally asked Lieutenant Byrnes for permission to begin surveillance of him as a suspect, and Byrnes naturally granted permission, and the tailing began that afternoon.

Never let it be said that policemen look with prejudice upon citizens who have previously been convicted of a crime.

Of the four guests in the Deaf Man's room at the Devon Hotel, three had previously been convicted of crimes. The fourth was a plain-looking woman in her late thirties, and she had never so much as received a parking ticket. The hotel was one of the city's lesser-known dumps, furnished economically and without imagination. There was only one easy chair in the room, and the men had graciously allowed the lady to claim it. They themselves sat on straight-backed wooden chairs facing a small end table that had been pulled up and placed within the semicircle they formed. A child's slate was propped up on the end table. The Deaf Man had served drinks (the lady had politely declined), and they sat sipping them thoughtfully as they examined the chalked diagram on the slate.

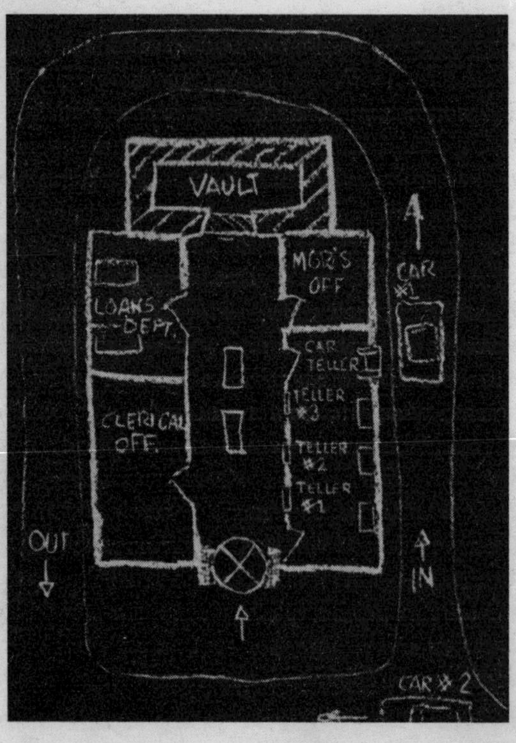

"Any questions?" the Deaf Man said.

"I've got one."

"Let's hear it, John."

John Preiss was a tall slender man with a pock-marked face. He was the only man in the room who had not dressed for the occasion. The others, as though attending a church social, were all wearing jackets and ties. John was wearing a cardigan sweater over an open-throated sports shirt. "Where's the alarm box?" he asked.

"I don't know," the Deaf Man answered. "It's not important. As I've told you before, I *expect* the alarm to be sounded."

"I don't like it," John said.

"Then this is the time to get out. None of you yet know where the bank is, or when we're going to hit. If anything about the job doesn't appeal to you, you're free to pass."

"I mean," John said, "if the damn alarm goes off . . ."

"It *will* go off, it *has* to go off. That's the least of our worries."

"Maybe you'd better explain it again, Mr. Taubman," the woman said.

"I'd be happy to, Angela," the Deaf Man replied. "Where shall I begin?"

"The beginning might be a good place," one of the other men said. He was portly, partially balding, chewing on a dead cigar. His name was Kerry Donovan.

"Very well," the Deaf Man said, and picked up a pointer from the end table. "This is the vault. Forget about getting into it any other way than through the door. The door is opened at eight-thirty every morning, and is not closed until the employees leave at close to five in the evening."

"What time do we hit?" Rudy Manello asked. He was younger than any of the others, a narrow-faced man, with brown hair combed straight back without a part. He was smoking a cigarette, the ash dangerously close to spilling all over the floor.

"I'll let you know the time and place as soon as we're all committed, Rudy."

"Why all the secrecy?" Rudy asked.

"I do not intend spending any amount of time in prison," the Deaf Man said, and smiled. "Whereas I trust you all implicitly, I must take certain precautions at this stage of the planning."

"So let's hear the plan again," Angela said, and crossed her legs, a move that had no visible effect on any of the men in the room. Angela Gould was perhaps the least attractive woman the Deaf Man had ever met. Long-nosed, thin-lipped, bespectacled, blessed with curly hair in an age that demanded sleekness, dumpy, with an irritating, whiny voice—impossible, utterly impossible. And yet perfect for the part she would play on the last day of April.

"Here is the plan again," the Deaf Man said, and smiled graciously. He did not much like any of the people he was forced to deal with, but even the best football coach needs a team to execute the plays. "On the day of the robbery, Kerry will enter the bank, carrying a rather large case in which there will be architectural plans and a scale model of a housing development for which he needs financing. He will previously have made an appointment with the manager, and he will be there ostensibly to show him the plans and the model."

"Where do we get this stuff?" Kerry asked.

"It is being prepared for us now. By a legitimate architectural firm that believes it to be a bona-fide land development project."

"Okay, go ahead."

"Once inside the manager's office, you will explain your project and then put your plans and your model on his desk, asking him to come around to your side of the desk so that he can read the plans better. You will do this in order to get him away from the alarm button, which is on the floor under his desk, and which he will be unable to reach from your side."

"I thought you *expected* the alarm to go off," John said.

"Yes, but not until we have the money."

"The money that's in the vault."

"Yes. As I've already told you, there will be five hundred thousand dollars in payroll money in the bank's vault. It will be necessary for Kerry to get *into* the vault . . ."

"That's the part I don't like," Kerry said.

"There will be no problem about getting into the vault, Kerry. The moment the manager comes around to your side of the desk, you will put a gun in his back and inform him that a holdup is in progress. You will also tell him that, unless he escorts you to the vault immediately, you will blow his brains out."

"That's exactly what bothers me," Kerry said. "Suppose he says, 'Go ahead, blow my brains out.' What do I do then?"

"The bank is insured. You will rarely find heroic bank employees nowadays. They all have instructions to press the alarm button and sit tight until the police arrive. In this case, we are depriving Mr. Alton—that's the manager's name—of the opportunity to sound the alarm. I can assure you he will not avail himself of the alternate opportunity—that of having his brains blown out. He will escort you to the vault, quietly and without fuss."

"I hope so," Kerry said. "But what if he doesn't? Since I'm the only guy inside the bank, I'm automatically the fall guy."

"I will also be inside the bank," the Deaf Man said.

"Yeah, but you won't be holding a gun on any manager."

"I chose you for the job because you'd had previous experience," the Deaf Man said. "I assumed you would have the nerve to . . ."

"Yeah, I got *caught* on my previous experience," Kerry said.

"Do you want the job or don't you?" the Deaf Man asked. "You can still get out. No hard feelings either way."

"Let me hear the rest of it again."

"You go into the vault with Mr. Alton, carrying your leather case, the architectural contents of which are now in Mr. Alton's office."

"In other words," Angela said, "the case is empty now."

"Precisely," the Deaf Man said, and thought, *Impossible.* "As soon as you are inside the vault, Kerry, you will transfer the payroll to your case, and then allow Mr. Alton to escort you back to his office . . ."

"Suppose there's somebody else in the vault when we get in there?"

"You will already have informed Mr. Alton that should anyone question your presence, he is to say you're there to test the alarm system. Presumably, that is why you are carrying a big black leather case."

"But suppose somebody's actually *in* the vault?" Kerry said. "You didn't answer the question."

"Mr. Alton will ask that person to leave. The testing of an alarm system is not something normally open to casual scrutiny by insignificant bank personnel."

"Okay. So I'm in the vault transferring all that money into my case . . ."

"Correct. The moment I see you *leaving* the vault to head back for Mr. Alton's office, I will step outside the bank and set the second phase of the plan in motion."

"This is where *we* come in," Angela said, and smiled.

Utterly impossible, the Deaf Man thought, and returned her smile.

"Yes," he said pleasantly enough, "this is where you come in. If you'll all look at the diagram again, you'll see that a driveway comes in off the street on the right of the bank, runs around the rear of the bank, and then emerges into the street again on the left. The driveway was put in to accommodate the car teller's window. It is only wide enough to permit passage of a single automobile. Two things will happen the moment I step out of the bank. First, John and Rudy, in Car Number One, will drive up to the teller's window. Second, Angela, in Car Number Two, will park across the mouth of the driveway, get out of the car, and open the hood as though searching for starter trouble."

"That's so no other cars can get in the driveway after Rudy and John pull up to the teller's window," Angela said.

"Yes," the Deaf Man answered blankly.

"Meanwhile," Kerry said, and the Deaf Man was pleased to see that he had managed to generate some sort of enthusiasm for the project, "*I'll* be in the manager's office, tying him up and sticking a gag in his mouth."

"Correct," the Deaf Man said. "John?"

"I'll get out of the car at the teller's window and smash the glass there with a sledge hammer."

"Which is precisely when the alarm will go off. You won't hear it. It's a silent alarm that sounds at the 86th Precinct and also at the Security Office."

"But *I'll* hear the glass smashing," Kerry said, and grinned. "Which is when I open the door leading from the manager's office to the tellers' cages, go through the gate in the counter, and jump through the busted window into the driveway."

"Yes," the Deaf Man said. "You get into the car, and Rudy, at the wheel, will drive around the rear of the bank and out into the street again. I will meanwhile have entered the car Angela is driving, and we will all go off together into a lucrative sunset."

"How long does it take the police to answer that alarm?" Rudy asked.

"Four minutes."

"How long does it take to drive around the bank?"

"A minute and a half."

The group was silent.

"What do you think?" the Deaf Man asked. He had deliberately chosen nonthinkers, and he fully realized that his task today was one of selling an idea. He looked at them hopefully. If he had not completely sold them, he would replace them. It was as simple as that.

"I think it'll work," John said.

"So do I," Rudy said.

"Oh, how can it miss?" Angela said in her whiny voice, and the Deaf Man winced.

"Kerry?" he asked.

Kerry, of course, was the key man. As he had rightfully pointed out, he was the only one of the group who would actually be *inside* the bank, holding a gun, committing a robbery. The question Kerry asked now was the only question he should have asked; the Deaf Man was beginning to think he had chosen someone altogether too smart.

"How come *you* don't go into the manager's office and stick the gun in his back?" Kerry asked.

"I'm known at the bank," the Deaf Man said.

"How?"

"As a depositor."

"Why can't a depositor also be somebody who's asking for financing on a housing development?"

"There's no reason why he couldn't be. But my face has been recorded by the bank's cameras many times already, and I don't wish to spend the rest of my life dodging the police."

"What about *my* face?" Kerry asked. "They'll know what I look like, won't they? What's to stop them from hounding *me* after the job?"

"*You'll* be in disguise."

"You didn't mention that."

"I know I didn't," the Deaf Man said. He hadn't mentioned it because he hadn't thought of it until just this moment. "You will grow a mustache and shave your head before the job. As far as they'll ever know, the bank was robbed by a Yul Brynner with a hairy lip." Everyone laughed, including Kerry. The Deaf Man waited. They were almost in his pocket. It all depended on Kerry.

Kerry, still laughing, shook his head in admiration. "I got to hand it to you," he said. "You think of everything." He took a long swallow of the drink, and said, "I don't know about the rest of you, but it sounds good to me." He raised his glass to the Deaf Man and said, "Count me in."

The Deaf Man did not mention to Kerry that his next logical question should have been, "Mr. Taubman, why don't *you* shave your head and grow a mustache?" or that he was extremely grateful to him for not having asked it. But then again, had the question come up, the Deaf Man would have thought of an answer. As Kerry had noted, the Deaf Man thought of everything, even when he *didn't* think of everything. Grinning now, he said to the others, "May I count *all* of you in?" and turned away not three seconds later to mix a fresh round of drinks in celebration.

The second photostat of the Japanese Zero came in the afternoon mail, just as Carella was leaving the squadroom. Carella studied it solemnly as Meyer tacked it to the bulletin board alongside the five other stats. Then he picked up the manila envelope in which it had been delivered and looked again at the typewritten address.

"He's still addressing them to me," he said.

"I see that."

"And still spelling my name wrong. It's Stephen with a *p-h*, not Steven with a *v*."

"*I* didn't even know that," Meyer said.

"Yeah," Carella said, and then turned to look at the row of stats again. "Do you suppose he knows I have twins?"

"Why?"

"Because that's all I can figure. He's addressing the stuff to me, he's putting it on an entirely personal level. So maybe he's also duplicating it because I have twins."

"You think so?"

"Yeah." Carella paused. "What do *you* think?"

"*I* think you're getting slightly paranoid," Meyer said.

Sanford Elliot was working when Carella went over with his search warrant. The long wooden table at which he sat was spattered with daubs of wax. A round biscuit tin was near his right elbow, half full of molten wax, a naked electric light bulb shining into its open top to keep it soft. Elliot dipped into the can with fingers or wire-end tool, adding, spreading, molding wax onto the small figure of the nude on the table before him. He was thoroughly engrossed in what he was doing, and did not look up when Carella walked into the studio from the front of the shop. Carella did not wish to startle him. The man might have figured in a murder, and a startled murderer is a dangerous one. He hesitated just inside the curtain that divided the studio from the front, and then coughed. Elliot looked up immediately.

"You," he said.

"Me," Carella answered.

"What is it this time?"

"Do you always work in wax, Mr. Elliot?"

"Only when I'm going to cast something in bronze."

"How do you mean?"

"I don't give art lessons," Elliot said abruptly. "What do you want?"

"This is what I want," Carella said, and walked to him and handed him the search warrant:

IN THE NAME OF THE PEOPLE OF THIS STATE TO ANY POLICE OFFICER IN THIS CITY:

Proof by affidavit having been made this day by Detective Stephen L. Carella that there is probable cause for believing that certain property constitutes evidence of the crime of murder or tends to show that a particular person has committed the crime of murder:

YOU ARE THEREFORE COMMANDED, between the hours of 6:00 A.M. and 9:00 P.M. to make an immediate search of the ground floor rear of premises 1211 King's Circle, occupied by Sanford Elliot and of the person of Sanford Elliot and of any other person who may be found to have such property in his possession or under his control or to whom such property may have been delivered, for a size twelve, right-footed, white tennis sneaker, and if you find such property or any part thereof to bring it before me at the Criminal Courts Building in this county.

This warrant must be executed within ten days of the date of issuance.

Elliot read the warrant, checked the date and the signature of the supreme court justice, and then said, "*What* sneaker? I don't know what you're talking about."

Carella looked down at his right foot. Elliot was no longer wearing the sneaker; instead, there was a leather sandal on his foot.

"You were wearing a sneaker the last time I saw you. That search warrant gives me the right to look for it."

"You're out of your mind," Elliot said.

"Am I?"

"I've never worn sneakers in my life."

"I'll just look around, if you don't mind."

"How can I stop you?" Elliot said sarcastically, and went back to work.

"Want to tell me about the wax?" Carella said. He was roaming the studio now, looking for a closet or a cupboard, the logical places one might put a sneaker. There was a second curtain hanging opposite the door leading to the shop, and Carella figured it might be covering the opening to a closet. He was mistaken. There was a small sink-refrigerator-stove unit behind the curtain. He stepped on the foot lever to open the refrigerator door and discovered that it was full of arms, legs, breasts, and heads. They had all been rendered in wax, to be sure, but the discovery was startling nonetheless, somewhat like stumbling upon the remains of a mass Lilliputian dismemberment. "What are these?" Carella said.

"Parts," Elliot answered. He had obviously decided not to be cooperative, responsive, or even polite. His attitude was not exactly surprising; his visitor had come into the studio with a piece of paper empowering him to go through the place from top to bottom.

"Did you mold them?"

"Yes," Elliot said.

"I suppose you keep them in here so they won't melt."

"Brilliant."

"Why do you keep them at all?"

"I made up a batch from rubber molds," Elliot said. "I use them as prototypes, changing them to fit a specific pose."

Carella nodded, closed the refrigerator, and began wandering the studio again. He found what he thought was a packing crate, but when he lifted the lid he discovered that Elliot stored his clothes in it. He kneeled and began going through the crate, being careful not to disturb the order in which blue jeans and sweaters, shirts and socks, underwear and jackets were arranged. A single sandal was in the crate, the mate to the one Elliot was now wearing. There were also two pairs of loafers. But no sneaker. Carella put the lid onto the crate again.

"Why do you model in wax if it's so perishable?" he asked.

"I told you, I only do it when I'm going to be casting in bronze." Elliot put down the wire-end tool in his hand, turned to Carella, and patiently said, "It's called *cire perdue,* the lost-wax method. A mold is made of the piece when it gets to the foundry, and then the wax is melted out, and molten bronze is poured into the mold."

"Then the original wax piece is lost, is that right?"

"Brilliant," Elliot said again, and picked up a fettling knife.

"What do you do when you get the bronze piece back?"

"Chisel or file off the fins, plug any holes, color it, polish it, and mount it on a marble base."

"What's in here?" Carella asked, indicating a closed door.

"Storage."

"Of what?"

"Larger pieces. Most of them in plaster."

"Mind if I take a look?"

"You're hot stuff, you know that?" Elliot said. "You come around with a search warrant, and then you go through the charade of asking me whether or not you can . . ."

"No sense being uncivilized about it, is there?"

"Why not? I thought you were investigating a murder."

"I didn't think you realized that, Mr. Elliot."

"I realize it fine. And I've already told you I don't know who the dead man . . ."

"Yes, you've already told me. The trouble is, I don't happen to believe you."

"Then don't be so fucking polite," Elliot said. "If I'm a murder suspect, I don't need your good manners."

Carella went into the storage room without answering. As Elliot had promised, the room contained several larger pieces, all done in plaster, all unmistakably of Mary Margaret Ryan. A locked door was at the far end of the room. "Where's that door go?" Carella asked.

"What?" Elliot said.

"The other door here."

"Outside. The alley."

"You want to unlock it for me, please?"

"I don't have a key. I never open that door. It's locked all the time."

"I'll have to kick it open then," Carella said.

"Why?"

"Because I want to see what's out in that alley."

"There's nothing out in that alley."

There were prints in the plaster dust on the floor. Easily identifiable prints left by someone's right foot; on either side of them, there were circular marks that might have been left by the rubber tips of crutches. The prints led directly to the alley door.

"What do you say, Elliot? Are you going to open it for me?"

"I told you I don't have a key."

"Fine," Carella said, and kicked the door in without another word.

"Are you allowed to do that?" Elliot said.

"Sue me," Carella said, and went out into the alley. A garbage can and two cardboard boxes full of trash were stacked against the brick wall. In one of the cardboard cartons Carella found the sneaker Elliot had been wearing yesterday. He came back into the studio, showed the sneaker to Elliot and said, "Ever see this before?"

"Never."

"I figured you wouldn't have," Carella said. "Mr. Elliot, at the risk of sounding like a television cop, I'd like to warn you not to leave the city."

"Where would I go?" Elliot asked.

"Who knows? You seem to have a penchant for Boston. Take my advice and stay put till I get back to you."

"What do you hope to get from a fucking moldy sneaker?" Elliot said.

"Maybe some wax that *didn't* get lost," Carella answered.

The cop who picked up the surveillance of Frederick Lipton at five o'clock that evening was Cotton Hawes. From his parked sedan across the street from the real estate office, he watched Lipton as he locked up the place and walked down the block to where his Ford convertible was parked. He followed him at a safe distance to a garden apartment a mile and a half from the real estate office, and waited outside for the next four hours, at which time Lipton emerged, got into his Ford again, and drove to a bar imaginatively named the Gee-Gee-Go-Go. Since Lipton had never met Hawes and did not know what he looked like, and also since the place advertised topless dancers, Hawes figured he might as well step inside and continue the surveillance there. The place was no more disappointing than he expected it to be. Topless dancing, in this city, was something more than topless—the something more being pasties or filmy brassieres. Hookers freely roamed the streets and plied their trade, but God forbid a mammary gland should be exposed to some unsuspecting visitor from Sioux City. The dancers, nonetheless, were usually young and attractive, gyrating wildly to canned rock music while the equivalent of front-row center in a burlesque house ogled them from stools lining the bar. Not so at the Gee-Gee-Go-Go. The dancers here were thirtyish or better, considerably over the hill for the kind of acrobatics they performed or the kind of erotic response they attempted to provoke. Hawes sat in bored silence while the elaborate electronics system buffeted him with waves of amplified sound and the dancers, four in all, came out in succession to grind away in tempo along the length of the bar. Keeping one eye on Lipton, who sat at the other end of the bar, Hawes speculated that the sound system had cost more than the dancing girls, but this was Calm's Point and not Isola; one settled for whatever he could get in the city's hinterlands.

Lipton seemed to know one of the dancers, a woman of about thirty-five, with bleached blond hair and siliconed breasts tipped with star-shaped pasties, ample buttocks, rather resembling in build one of the sturdy Clydesdale horses in the Rheingold commercials. When she finished her number, she kneeled down beside him on the bar top, chatted with him briefly, and then went to join him at a table in the rear of the place. Lipton ordered a drink for the girl, and they talked together for perhaps a half hour, at the end of which time she clambered onto the bar top again to hurl some more beef at her audience, all of whom watched her every move in pop-eyed fascination, as though privileged to be witnessing Markova at a command performance of *Swan Lake*. Lipton settled his bill and left the bar. Without much regret, Hawes followed him back to the garden apartment, where he put his car into one of a row of single garages on the ground level of the building, and then went upstairs. Figuring he was home for the night, Hawes drove back to the Gee-Gee-Go-Go, ordered a scotch and soda, and waited for an opportunity to engage the beefy blonde in conversation.

He caught her after she finished her number, a tiresome repetition of the last three, or five, or fifty numbers she had performed on the bar top. She was heading either for the ladies' room or a dressing room behind the bar when he stepped into her path, smiled politely, and said, "I like the way you dance. May I buy you a drink?"

The girl said, "Sure," without hesitation, confirming his surmise that part of the job was getting the customers to buy watered-down booze or ginger ale masquerading as champagne. She led him to the same table Lipton had shared with her, where a waiter appeared with something like lightning speed, pencil poised. The girl ordered a double bourbon and soda; apparently the champagne dodge was a mite too sophisticated for the Calm's Point sticks. Hawes ordered a scotch and soda and then smiled at the girl and said, "I really do like the way you dance. Have you been working here long?"

"Are you a cop?" the girl asked.

"No," Hawes said, startled.

"Then what are you? A crook?"

"No."

"Then why are you carrying a gun?" the girl said.

Hawes cleared his throat. "Who says I am?"

"*I* say you are. On your right hip. I saw the bulge when we were talking in the hallway there, and I brushed against it when we were coming over to the table. It's a gun, all right."

"It's a gun, yes."

"So, *are* you a cop?"

"No. Close to it, though," Hawes said.

"Yeah? What does that mean? Private eye?"

"I'm a night watchman. Factory over on Klein and Sixth."

"If you're a night watchman, what are you doing here? This is the nighttime."

"I don't start till midnight."

"You always drink like this before you go to work?"

"Not always."

"Where'd you go when you left here before?" the girl asked.

"You noticed me, huh?" Hawes answered, and grinned, figuring he'd get the conversation onto a socio-sexual level and move it away from more dangerous ground.

"I noticed," the girl said, and shrugged. "You're a big guy. Also you've got red hair, which is unusual. Do they call you 'Red'?"

"They call me Hamp."

"Hamp? What kind of name is that?"

"Short for Hampton."

"Is that your first name or your last?"

"My last. It's Oliver Hampton."

"I can see why you settled for Hamp."

"What's *your* name?"

"It's on the card outside. Didn't you see it?"

"I guess I missed it."

"Rhonda Spear."

"Is that your real name?"

"It's my show business name."

"What's your real name?"

"Why do you want to know? So you can call me up in the middle of the night and breathe on the phone?"

"I might call you, but I wouldn't breathe."

"If a person doesn't breathe, he drops dead," Rhonda said. She smiled, consumed her drink in a single swallow, and said, "I'd like another double bourbon, please."

"Sure," Hawes said, and signaled for the waiter to bring another round. "How many of those do you drink in a night?"

"Ten or twelve," she said. "It's only Coca-Cola," she said. "You're a cop, you know damn well it's Coca-Cola."

"I'm not a cop, and I didn't know it was Coca-Cola," Hawes said.

"*I* know cops," Rhonda said. "And *you* know Coca-Cola." She hesitated, looked him straight in the eye, and said, "What do you want from me, officer?"

"Little conversation, that's all," Hawes said.

"About what?"

"About why you would tell a cop, if that's what you think I am, that he's paying for bourbon and getting Coca-Cola."

Rhonda shrugged. "Why not? If this joint was gonna be busted, they'd have done it ages ago. Everybody in this precinct, from the lieutenant on down, is on the take. We even dance without the pasties every now and then. Nobody ever bothers us. Is that why you're here, officer," she asked sweetly, "to get your share of the pie?"

"I'm not a cop," Hawes said, "and I wouldn't care if you danced bare-assed while drinking a whole crate of Coca-Cola."

Rhonda laughed, suddenly and girlishly. Her mirth transformed her face, revealing a fleeting glimpse of what she must have looked like when she was a lot younger, and a lot softer. The laughter trailed, the image died. "Thanks, honey," she said to the waiter, and lifted her glass and said to Hawes, "Maybe you're *not* a cop, after all. Who gives a damn?"

"Cheers," Hawes said.

"Cheers," she answered, and they both drank. "So if you're not a cop, what do you want from me?"

"You're a pretty woman," Hawes said.

"Um-huh."

"I'm sure you know that," he said, and lowered his eyes in a swift covetous sweep of the swelling star-tipped breasts.

"Um-huh."

"Saw you talking to a guy earlier. I'm sure he . . ."

"You did, huh?"

"Sure."

"You've been watching me, huh?"

"Sure. And I'll bet *he* didn't want to talk about the price of Coca-Cola, either."

"How do *you* know what he wanted to talk about?"

"I don't. I'm just saying that a pretty woman like you . . ."

"Um-huh."

"Must get a lot of attention from men. So you shouldn't be so surprised by *my* attention. That's all," he said, and shrugged.

"You're kind of cute," Rhonda said. "It's a shame."

"What is?"

"That you're a cop."

"Look, how many times . . ."

"You're a cop," she said flatly. "I don't know what you're after, but something tells me to say good night. Whatever you are, you're trouble."

"I'm a night watchman," Hawes said.

"Yeah," Rhonda replied. "And I'm Lillian Gish." She swallowed the remainder of her drink, said, "You'll settle with the waiter, huh?" and swiveled away from the table, ample buttocks threatening the purple satin shorts she wore.

Hawes paid for the drinks, and left.

On Saturday morning, while Carella was waiting for a lab report on the sneaker he had found in Elliot's trash, he made a routine check of the three hospitals in the area, trying to discover if and when a man named Sanford Elliot had been treated for a sprained ankle. The idea of calling all the private physicians in the area was out of the question, of course; if Carella had not hit pay dirt with one of the hospitals, he would have given up this line of investigation at once. But sometimes you get lucky. On Saturday, April 24, Carella got lucky on the second call he made.

The intern on duty in the Emergency Room of Buenavista Hospital was a Japanese named Dr. Yukio Watanabe. He told Carella that business was slow at the moment and that he was free to check through the log; had Carella called an hour ago, he'd have been told to buzz off fast because the place had been thronged with victims of a three-car highway accident.

"You never saw so much blood in your life," Watanabe said, almost gleefully, Carella thought. "Anyway, what period are you interested in? I've got the book right here in front of me."

"This would have been sometime between the eighth and fifteenth," Carella said.

"Of this month?"

"Yes."

"Okay, let's take a look. What'd you say his name was?"

"Sanford Elliot."

There was a long silence on the line. Carella waited.

"I'm checking," Watanabe said. "Sprained ankle, huh?"

"That's right."

"Nothing so far."

"Where are you?"

"Through the eleventh," Watanabe said, and fell silent again.

Carella waited.

"Nothing," Watanabe said at last. "You sure it was between those dates?"

"Could you check a bit further for me?"

"How far?"

"Through the next week, if you've got time."

"We've always got time here until somebody comes in with a broken head," Watanabe said. "Okay, here we go. Sanford Elliot, right?"

"Right."

Watanabe was silent. Carella could hear him turning pages.

"Sanford Elliot," Watanabe said. "Here it is."

"When did he come in?"

"Monday morning, April nineteenth."

"What time?"

"Ten past seven. Treated by Dr. Goldstein." Watanabe paused. "I thought you said it was a sprained ankle."

"Wasn't it?"

"Not according to this. He was treated for third-degree burns. Foot, ankle, and calf of the left leg."

"I see," Carella said.

"Does that help you?"

"It confuses me. But thanks, anyway."

"No problem," Watanabe said, and hung up.

Carella stared at the telephone. It was always good to stare at the telephone when you didn't have any ideas. There was something terribly reassuring about the knowledge that the telephone itself was worthless until a bell started ringing. Carella waited for a bell to start ringing. Instead, Miscolo came in with the morning mail.

The lady was lovely, to be sure, but nobody knew who she was. There was no question about *what* she was. She was a silent film star. There is a look about silent film stars that immediately identifies their profession and their era, even to people who have never watched any of their films. None of the detectives looking at the lady's picture were old enough to have seen her films, but they knew immediately what she was, and so they began riffling through their memories, calling up ancient names and trying to associate them with printed photographs they'd seen accompanying articles probably titled "Whatever Happened To?"

"Gloria Swanson?" Hawes asked.

"No, I know what Gloria Swanson looks like," Meyer said. "This is definitely not Gloria Swanson."

"Dolores Del Rio?" Hawes said.

"No, Dolores Del Rio was very sexy," Carella said. "Still *is*, as a matter of fact. I saw a recent picture of her only last month."

"What's the matter with *this* girl?" Meyer said. "I happen to think *this* girl is very sexy."

"Norma Talmadge, do you think?" Hawes said.

"Who's Norma Talmadge?" Kling asked.

"Get this bottle baby out of here, will you?" Meyer said.

"I mean it, who's Norma Talmadge?"

"How about Marion Davies?"

"I don't think so," Carella said.

"Who's Marion Davies?" Kling asked, and Meyer shook his head.

"Janet Gaynor?" Hawes said.

"No."

"Pola Negri?"

"I know who Pola Negri is," Kling said. "The Vamp."

"Theda Bara was The Vamp," Meyer said.

"Oh," Kling said.

"Dolores Costello?"

"No, I don't think so."

"Mae Murray?"

"No."

The telephone rang. Hawes picked up the receiver. "87th Squad," he said, "Detective Hawes." He listened silently for a moment, and then said, "Hold on, will you? I think you want Carella." He handed the receiver to him, and said, "It's the lab. They've got a report on your tennis sneaker."

Through the plate-glass window of Sandy Elliot's shop, Carella could see him inside with two bikies. He recognized one of them as Yank, the cigar-smoking heavyweight he had spoken to on Tuesday. Yank was wandering around the shop, examining the pieces of sculpture, paying scant attention to Elliot and the second bikie, who was wagging his finger in Elliot's face like a district attorney in a grade-C flick. Elliot leaned on his crutches and listened solemnly to what was being said, occasionally nodding. At last the second bikie turned away from the counter, tapped Yank on the arm, and started out of the shop. Carella moved swiftly into the adjacent doorway. As the pair passed by, he caught a quick glimpse of Yank's companion—short, brawny, with a pock-marked face and a sailor's rolling gait, the name "Ox" lettered on the front of his jacket. As they went off, Carella heard Yank burst into laughter.

He waited several moments, came out of the doorway, and went into Elliot's shop.

"See you had a couple of art lovers in here," he said. "Did they buy anything?"

"No."

"What did they want?"

"What do *you* want?" Elliot said.

"Some answers," Carella said.

"I've given you all the answers I've got."

"I haven't given you all the questions yet."

"Maybe you'd better advise me of my rights first."

"This is a field investigation, and you haven't been taken into custody or otherwise detained, so please don't give me any bullshit about rights. Nobody's violating your rights. I've got a few simple questions, and I want a few simple answers. How about it, Elliot? I'm investigating a homicide here."

"I don't know anything about any homicide."

"Your sneaker was found at the scene of the crime."

"Who says so?"

"*I* say so. And the police lab says so. How did it get there, Elliot?"

"I have no idea. I threw that pair of sneakers out two weeks ago. Somebody must've picked one of them out of the trash."

"When *I* picked it out of the trash yesterday, you said you'd never seen it before. You can't have it both ways, Elliot. Anyway, you couldn't have thrown them out two weeks ago, because I saw you wearing one of them only two *days* ago. What do you say? You going to play ball, or do you want to take a trip to the station house?"

"For what? You going to charge me with murder?"

"Maybe."

"I don't think you will," Elliot said. "I'm not a lawyer, but I know you can't build a case on a sneaker you found in a goddamn abandoned tenement."

"How do *you* know where we found that sneaker?"

"I read about the murder in the papers."

"How do you know which murder I'm investigating?"

"You showed me a picture, didn't you? It doesn't take a mastermind to tie the newspaper story to . . ."

"Get your hat, Elliot. I'm taking you to the station house."

"You can't arrest me," Elliot said. "Who the hell do you think you're kidding? You've got nothing to base a charge on."

"Haven't I?" Carella said. "Try this for size. It's from the Code of Criminal Procedure. *A peace officer may, without a warrant, arrest a person when he has reasonable cause for believing that a felony has been committed, and that the person arrested has committed it . . .*"

"On the basis of a *sneaker?*" Elliot said.

"Though it should afterwards appear," Carella continued, *"that no felony has been committed, or, if committed, that the person arrested did not commit it.* All right, Elliot, I *know* a felony was committed on the night of April eighteenth, and I *know* an article of clothing belonging to you was found at the scene of the crime, and that's reasonable cause for believing you were there either before or after it happened. Either way, I think I've got justifiable cause for arrest. Would you like to tell me how you sprained your ankle? Or is it a torn Achilles tendon?"

"It's a sprained ankle."

"Want to tell me about it? Or shall we save it for the squadroom?"

"I would not like to tell you anything. And if you take me to the squadroom, you'll be forced to advise me of my rights. Once you do that, I'll refuse to answer any questions, and . . ."

"We'll worry about that when we get there."

"You're wasting your time, Carella, and you know it."

The men stared at each other. There was a faintly superior smirk on Elliot's mouth, a confident challenge in his eyes. Against his better judgment, Carella decided to pick up the gauntlet.

"Your ankle *isn't* sprained," he said. "Buenavista Hospital reports having treated you for third-degree burns on April nineteenth, the morning after the murder."

"I've never been to Buenavista Hospital in my life."

"Then someone's been using your name around town, Elliot."

"Maybe so."

"You want to unwrap that bandage and show me your foot?"

"No."

"Am I going to need another warrant?"

"Yes. Why don't you just go get yourself one?"

"There were remains of a small fire in one of the rooms . . ."

"Go get your warrant. I think we're finished talking."

"Is that where you had your accident, Elliot? Is that where you burned your foot?"

"I've got nothing more to say to you."

"Okay, have it your way," Carella said angrily, and opened the front door. "I'll be back."

He slammed the door shut behind him and went out onto the street, no closer to a solution than he had been when he walked into the shop. There were three incontrovertible facts that added up to evidence of a sort, but unfortunately not *enough* evidence for an arrest. The sneaker found in that tenement was unquestionably Elliot's. It had been found in the corner of a room that contained the dead ashes of a recent fire. And Elliot had been treated for burns on April 19, the morning after the murder. Carella had hoped Elliot might be intimidated by these three seemingly related facts, and then either volunteer a confession or blurt out something that would move the investigation onto firmer ground. But Elliot had called the bluff. A charge on the basis of the existing evidence alone would be kicked out of court in three minutes flat. Moreover, Elliot's rights were securely protected; if arrested, he would have to be warned against saying anything self-incriminating, and would undoubtedly refuse to answer any questions without an attorney present. Once a lawyer entered the squadroom, he would most certainly advise Elliot to remain silent, which would take them right back to where they'd started: a charge of murder based on evidence that indicated only possible presence at the scene of a crime.

Carella walked rapidly toward his parked car.

He was certain of only one thing: if Sanford Elliot *really* knew nothing at all about what had happened on the fifth floor of 433 North Harrison on the night of April 18, he would be answering any and all questions willingly and honestly. But he was *not* answering willingly, and he was lying whenever he *did* answer. Which brought Carella to the little lady with the long brown hair, the frightened brown eyes, and the face of an angel—Mary Margaret Ryan, as sweet a young lass as had ever crossed herself in the anonymous darkness of a confessional. Mary Margaret Ryan, bless her soul, had told Carella that she and Elliot had come down from Boston late Monday night. But Elliot's foot had been treated at Buenavista on Monday *morning*. Which meant that Mary Margaret perhaps had something to tell her priest the next time she saw him. In the meantime, seeing as how Mary Margaret was a frightened, slender little wisp of a thing, Carella decided it was worth trying to frighten her a hell of a lot more.

He slammed the door of his car, stuck the key into the ignition switch, and started the engine.

The trouble was, Kling could not stop staring at her.

He had picked up Augusta at six o'clock sharp, and whereas she had warned him about the way she might look after a full day's shooting, she looked nothing less than radiant. Red hair still a bit damp (she confessed to having caught a quick shower in Jerry Bloom's own executive washroom), she came into the reception room to meet Kling, extended her hand to him, and then offered her cheek for a kiss he only belatedly realized was expected. Her cheek was cool and smooth, there was not a trace of makeup on her face except for the pale green shadow on her eyelids, the brownish liner just above her lashes. Her hair was brushed straight back from her forehead, falling to her shoulders without a part. She was wearing blue jeans, sandals, and a ribbed jersey top without a bra. A blue leather bag was slung over her right shoulder, but she shifted it immediately to the shoulder opposite, looped her right hand through his arm, and said, "Were you waiting long?"

"No, I just got here."

"Is something wrong?"

"No. What do you mean?"

"The way you're looking at me."

"No. No, no, everything's fine."

But he could not stop staring at her. The film they went to see was *Bullitt*, which Kling had seen the first time it played the circuit, but which Augusta was intent on seeing in the presence of a *real* cop. Kling hesitated to tell her that, real cop or not, the first time he'd seen *Bullitt* he hadn't for a moment known what the hell was going on. He had come out of the theater grateful that he hadn't been the cop assigned to the case, partially because he wouldn't have known where to begin unraveling it, and partially because fast car rides made him dizzy. He didn't know what the movie was about *this* time either, but not because of any devious motivation or complicated plot twists. The simple fact was that he didn't *watch* the picture; he watched Augusta instead. It was dark when they came out into the street. They walked in silence for several moments, and then Augusta said, "Listen, I think we'd better get something straight right away."

"What's that?" he said, afraid she would tell him she was married, or engaged, or living with a high-priced photographer.

"I *know* I'm beautiful," she said.

"What?" he said.

"Bert," she said, "I'm a model, and I get *paid* for being beautiful. It makes me very nervous to have you staring at me all the time."

"Okay, I won't . . ."

"No, please let me finish . . ."

"I thought you *were* finished."

"No. I want to get this settled."

"It's settled," he said. "Now we *both* know you're beautiful." He hesitated just an instant, and then added, "And modest besides."

"Oh, boy," she said. "I'm trying to relate as a goddamn *person,* and you're . . ."

"I'm sorry I made you uncomfortable," he said. "But the truth is . . ."

"Yes, what's the truth?" Augusta said. "Let's at least *start* with the truth, okay?"

"The truth is I've never in my life been out with a girl as beautiful as you are, that's the truth. And I can't get over it. So I keep staring at you. That's the truth."

"Well, you'll have to get over it."

"Why?"

"Because I think you're beautiful, too," Augusta said, "and we'd have one hell of a relationship if all we did was sit around and *stare* at each other all the time."

She stopped dead in the middle of the sidewalk. Kling searched her face, hoping she would recognize that this was not the same as staring.

"I mean," she said, "I expect we'll be seeing a lot of each other, and I'd like to think I'm permitted to *sweat* every now and then. I *do* sweat, you know."

"Yes, I suppose you do," he said, and smiled.

"Okay?" she said.

"Okay."

"Let's eat," she said. "I'm famished."

It was Detective-Lieutenant Peter Byrnes himself who identified the photostat of the silent silver-screen star. This was only reasonable, since he was the oldest man on the squad.

"This is Vilma Banky," he said.

"Are you sure?" Meyer asked.

"Positive. I saw her in *The Awakening,* and I also saw her in *Two Lovers* with Ronald Colman." Byrnes cleared his throat. "I was, naturally, a very small child at the time."

"Naturally," Meyer said.

"Banky," Hawes said. "He can't be that goddamn corny, can he?"

"What do you mean?" Byrnes said.

"He isn't telling us it's a *bank,* is he?"

"I'll bet he is," Meyer said. "Of course he is."

"I'll be damned," Byrnes said. "Put it up there on the bulletin board with the rest of them, Meyer. Let's see what else we've got here." He watched as Meyer tacked the picture to the end of the row. Two of Hoover, two of Washington, two of a Japanese Zero, and now Miss Banky. "All right, let's dope it out," Byrnes said.

"It's her last name," Hawes said. "Maybe we're supposed to put together all the last names."

"Yeah," Meyer said. "And come up with the name of the bank."

"Right, right."

"Hoover Washington Zero Bank," Byrnes said. "That's *some* bank."

"Or maybe the first names," Hawes suggested.

"John George Japanese Bank," Byrnes said. "Even better."

The men looked at the photostats and then looked at each other.

"Listen, let's not . . ."

"Right, right."

"He's not that smart. If *he* doped it out, *we* can dope it out."

"Right."

"So it isn't the last names, and it isn't the first names."

"So what is it?" Byrnes said.

"I don't know," Hawes said.

"Anyway, Cotton, he *is* that smart," Meyer said.

"That's right, he is," Byrnes said.

The men looked at the photostats again.

"J. Edgar Hoover," Hawes said.

"Right."

"Director of the FBI."

"Right."

"George Washington."

"Right, right."

"Father of the country."

"Which gives us nothing," Byrnes said.

"Zero," Meyer said.

"Exactly," Byrnes said.

"Let's start from the beginning," Hawes said. "The first picture we got was Hoover's, right?"

"Mmm."

"And then Washington and the Zero," Meyer said.

"All right, let's associate," Hawes said.

"What?"

"Let's free-associate. What do you think of when I say Washington?"

"General."

"President."

"Martha."

"Mount Vernon."

"D.C."

"State of."

"Let's take it back. General."

"Revolution."

"Valley Forge."

"Delaware."

"Cherry tree," Meyer said.

"Cherry tree?"

"He chopped down a cherry tree, didn't he?"

"How about President? What can we get from that?"

"Chief Executive."

"Commander in Chief."

"We're getting no place," Byrnes said.

"How about Hoover?"

"FBI."

"Federal Bureau of . . ."

"Federal!" Hawes said, and snapped his fingers. "A *federal* bank!"

"Yes," Byrnes said, and nodded, and the men fell silent.

"A federal bank in Washington?"

"Then why bother us with it?"

"What about the Zero?"

"Never mind the Zero, let's get back to Washington."

"No, wait a minute, maybe the Zero's important."

"How?"

"I don't know."

"Let's try it. Zero."

"Nothing."

"Goose egg."

"Zip."

"Zed."

"Zed?"

"Isn't that what they say in England?"

"For zero? I don't think so."

"Zero, zero . . ."

"Zero, one, two, three, four . . ."

"Love," Meyer said.

"Love?"

"That's zero in a tennis match."

"Let's get back to Washington."

"It *has* to be a federal bank in Washington," Byrnes said.

"Then why send us a picture of Washington himself? If he's trying to identify a *place* . . ."

"A bank *is* a place, isn't it?"

"Yes, but wouldn't it have been easier to send a picture of the White House or the Capitol dome or . . ."

"Who says he's trying to make it easy?"

"All right, let's see what we've got so far, all right? Federal Washington Zero Bank."

"Come on, Cotton, that doesn't make any sense at all."

"I know it doesn't, but that's the order they arrived in, so maybe . . ."

"Who says there has to be any special order?"

"Bank came last, didn't it?"

"Yes, but . . ."

"So that's where I've put it. Last."

"And Hoover came first," Meyer said. "So what?"

"So that's where I've put him."

"Federal Washington Zero Bank. It still doesn't make sense."

"Suppose the Zero means nothing at all? Literally zero. Suppose it's just there to be canceled out?"

"Try it."

"Federal Washington Bank."

"That's just what I said," Byrnes said. "A federal bank in Washington."

"If the bank's in Washington, why's he telling us about it?"

"Washington," Hawes said.

"Here we go again," Meyer said.

"Washington."

"President?"

"Federal President Bank?"

"No, no."

"General?"

"Federal General Bank?"

"Federal *Martha* Bank?"

"What the hell *was* he besides a general and the first President of the United . . ."

"First Federal Bank," Meyer said.

"What?"

"First *President,* First goddamn Federal *Bank!"*

"That's it," Byrnes said.

"That's *got* to be it."

"First Federal Bank," Meyer said, grinning.

"Get the phone book," Byrnes said.

They were all quite naturally proud of the deductive reasoning that had led them to their solution. They now felt they knew the name of the bank as well as the exact date of the planned holdup. Gleefully, they began going through the Yellow Pages, confident that the rest would be simple.

There were twenty-one First Federal Banks in Isola alone, and none of them were located in the 87th Precinct.

There were seventeen First Federals in Calm's Point.

There were nine in Riverhead, twelve in Majesta, and two in Bethtown, for a grand total of sixty-one banks.

It is sometimes not so good to work in a very big city.

Sunday.

Take a look at this city.

How can you possibly hate her?

She is composed of five sections as alien to each other as foreign countries with a common border; indeed, many residents of Isola are more familiar with the streets of England or France than they are with those of Bethtown, a stone's throw across the river. Her natives, too, speak dissimilar tongues. It is not uncommon for a Calm's Point accent to sound as unintelligible as the sounds a Welshman makes.

How can you hate this untidy bitch?

She is all walls, true. She flings up buildings like army stockades designed for protection against an Indian population long since cheated and departed. She hides the sky. She blocks her rivers from view. (Never perhaps in the history of mankind has a city so neglected the beauty of her waterways or treated them so casually. Were her rivers lovers, they would surely be unfaithful.) She forces you to catch glimpses of herself in quick takes, through chinks in long canyons, here a wedge of water, there a slice of sky, never a panoramic view, always walls enclosing, constricting, yet how can you hate her, this flirtatious bitch with smoky hair?

She's noisy and vulgar; there are runs in her nylons, and her heels are round (you can put this lady on her back with a kind word or a knowing leer because she's a sucker for attention, always willing to please, anxious to prove she's at least as good as most). She sings too fucking loud. Her lipstick is smeared across her face like an obscene challenge. She raises her skirt or drops it with equal abandon, she snarls, she belches, she bustles, she farts, she staggers, she falls, she's common, vile, treacherous, dangerous, brittle, vulnerable, stupid, obstinate, clever, and cheap, but it is impossible to hate her because when she steps out of the shower smelling of gasoline and sweat and smoke and grass and wine and flowers and food and dust and death (never mind the high-pollution level), she wears that blatant stink like the most expensive perfume. If you were born in a city, and raised in a city, you know the scent and it makes you dizzy. Not the scent of all the half-ass towns, hamlets, and villages that pose as cities and fool no one but their own hick inhabitants. There are half a dozen *real* cities in the world, and this is one of them, and it's impossible to hate her when she comes to you with a suppressed female giggle about to burst on her silly face, bubbling up from some secret adolescent well to erupt in merriment on her unpredictable mouth. (If you can't personalize a city, you have never lived in one. If you can't get romantic and sentimental about her, you're a foreigner still learning the language. Try Philadelphia, you'll love it there.) To know a real city, you've got to hold her close or not at all. You've got to breathe her.

Take a look at this city.

How can you possibly hate her?

The Sunday comics have been read and the apartment is still.

The man sitting in the easy chair is black, forty-seven years old, wearing an undershirt, denim trousers, and house slippers. He is a slender man, with brown eyes too large for his face, so that he always looks either frightened or astonished. There is a mild breeze blowing in off the fire escape, where the man's eight-year-old daughter has planted four o'clocks in a cheese box as part of a school project. The balmy feel of the day reminds the man that summer is coming. He frowns. He is suddenly upset, but he does not know quite why. His wife is next door visiting with a neighbor woman, and he feels neglected all at once, and begins wondering why she isn't preparing lunch for him, why she's next door gabbing when he's beginning to get hungry and summer is coming.

He gets out of the easy chair, sees perhaps for the hundredth time that the upholstery is worn in spots, the batting revealed. He sighs heavily. Again, he does not know why he is agitated. He looks down at the linoleum. The pattern has been worn off by the scuffings of years, and he stares at the brownish-red underlay and wonders where the bright colors went. He thinks he will turn on the television set and watch a baseball game, but it is too early yet, the game will not start until later in the day. He does not know what he wants to do with himself. And summer is coming.

He works in a toilet, this man.

He has a little table in a toilet in one of the hotels downtown. There is a white cloth on the table. There is a neat pile of hand towels on the table. There is a comb and a brush on the table. There is a dish in which the man puts four quarters when he begins work, in the hope that the tips he receives from male urinators will be at least as generous. He does not mind the work so much in the wintertime. He waits while his customers urinate, and then he hands them fresh towels, and he brushes off their coats and tries not to appear as if he is waiting for a tip. Most of the men tip him. Some of them do not. He goes home each night with toilet smells in his nostrils, and sometimes he is awakened by the rustling of rats in the empty hours, and the stench is still there, and he goes into the bathroom and puts salt into the palm of his hand and dilutes it with water and sniffs it up into his nose, but the smell will not go away.

In the winter, he does not mind the job too much.

In the summer, in his airless cubicle stinking of the waste of other men, he wonders whether he will spend the rest of his life unfolding towels, extending them to strangers, brushing coats, and waiting hopefully for quarter tips, trying not to look anxious, trying not to show on his face that those quarters are all that stand between him and welfare, all that stand between him and the loss of whatever shred of human dignity he still possesses.

Summer is coming.

He stands bleakly in the middle of the living room and listens to the drip of the water tap in the kitchen.

When his wife comes into the apartment some ten minutes later, he beats her senseless, and then holds her body close to his, and rocks her, keening, keening, rocking her, and still not knowing why he is agitated, or why he has tried to kill the one person on earth he loves.

In the April sunshine four fat men sit at a chess table in the park across the street from the university. All four of the men are wearing dark cardigan sweaters. Two of the men are playing chess, and two of them are kibitzing, but the game has been going on for so many Sundays now that it seems almost as though they are playing four-handed, the players and the kibitzers indistinguishable one from the other.

The white boy who enters the park is seventeen years old. He is grinning happily. He walks with a jaunty stride, and he sucks deep draughts of good spring air into his lungs, and he looks at the girls in their abbreviated skirts, and admires their legs, and feels horny and alive and masculine and strong.

When he comes abreast of the chess table where the old men are in deep concentration, he suddenly whirls and sweeps his hand across the table top, knocking the chess men to the ground. Grinning, he walks off, and the old men sigh and pick up the pieces and prepare to start the game all over again, though they know the one important move, the crucial move, has been lost to them forever.

The afternoon dawdles.

It is Sunday, the tempo of the city is lackadaisical. Grover Park has been closed to traffic, and cyclists pedal along the winding paths through banks of forsythia and cornelian cherry. A young girl's laughter carries for blocks. How can you possibly hate this city with her open empty streets stretching from horizon to horizon?

They are sitting on opposite sides of the cafeteria table. The younger one is wearing a turtleneck sweater and blue jeans. The older one is wearing a dark blue suit over a white shirt open at the throat, no tie. They are talking in hushed voices.

"I'm sorry," the one in the suit says. "But what can I do, huh?"

"Well, yeah, I know," the younger one answers. "I thought . . . since it's so close, you know?"

"Close, Ralphie, but no cigar."

"Well, only two bucks short is all, Jay."

"Two bucks is two bucks."

"I thought maybe just this once."

"I'd help you if I could, Ralphie, but I can't."

"Because I plan to go see my mother tomorrow, you know, and she's always good for a hit."

"Go see her tonight."

"Yeah, I would, only she went out to Sands Spit. We got people out there. My father drove her out there this morning."

"Then go see her tomorrow. And after you see her, you can come see me."

"Yeah, Jay, but . . . I'm starting to feel sick, you know?"

"That's too bad, Ralphie."

"Oh, sure, listen, I know it ain't your fault."

"You *know* it ain't."

"I know, I know."

"I'm in business, same as anybody else."

"Of course you are, Jay. Am I saying you ain't? Am I asking you for freebies? If it wasn't so close, I wouldn't ask you at all."

"Two dollars ain't close."

"Maybe for strangers it ain't, Jay. But we know each other a long time, ain't that true?"

"That's true."

"I'm a good customer, Jay. You know that."

"I know that."

"You carry me till tomorrow, Jay . . ."

"I can't, Ralphie. I just can't do it. If I did it for you, I'd have to do it for everybody on the street."

"Who'd know? I wouldn't tell a soul. I swear to God."

"Word gets around. Ralphie, you're a nice guy, I mean that from the bottom of my heart. But I can't help you. If I knew you didn't have the bread, I wouldn't even have come to meet you. I mean it."

"Yeah, but it's only two bucks."

"Two bucks here, two bucks there, it adds up. Who takes the risks, Ralphie, you or me?"

"Well, you, sure. But . . ."

"So now you're asking me to lay the stuff on you free."

"I'm *not*. I'm asking you to carry me till tomorrow when I get the bread from my old lady. That's all."

"I'm sorry."

"Jay? Jay, listen, have I ever asked you before? Have I ever once come to you and *not* had the bread? Tell the truth."

"No, that's true."

"Have I ever complained when I got stuck with shit that wasn't . . ."

"Now wait a minute, you never got no bad stuff from me. Are you trying to say I laid bad stuff on you?"

"No, no. Who said that?"

"I thought that's what you said."

"No, no."

"Then what did you say?"

"I meant when the stuff was bad all *over* the city. When the heat was on. Last June. You remember last June? When it was so hard to get anything halfway decent? That's what I meant."

"Yeah, I remember last June."

"I'm saying I never complained. When things were bad, I mean. I never complained."

"So?"

"So help me out this once, Jay, and . . ."

"I can't, Ralphie."

"Jay? Please."

"I can't."

"Jay?"

"No, Ralphie. Don't ask me."

"I'll get the money tomorrow, I swear to God."

"No."

"I'll see my mother tomorrow . . ."

"No."

"And get the money for you. Okay? What do you say, huh?"

"I got to split, Ralphie. You go see your mother . . ."

"Jay, please. Jay, I'm sick, I mean it. Please."

"See your mother, get the money . . ."

"Jay, please!

"And *then* talk to me, okay?"

"Jay!"

"So long, Ralphie."

• • •

Dusk moves rapidly over the city, spreading through the sky above Calm's Point to fill with guttering purple the crevices between chimney pot and spire. Flickers of yellow appear in window slits, neon tubes burst into oranges and blues, race around the shadowed sides of buildings to swallow their sputtering tails. Traffic signals blink in fiercer reds and brighter greens, emboldened by the swift descent of darkness. Color claims the night. It is impossible to hate this glittering nest of gems.

The patrolman does not know what to do.

The woman is hysterical, and she is bleeding from a cut over her left eye, and he does not know whether he should first call an ambulance or first go upstairs to arrest the man who hit her. The sergeant solves his dilemma, fortuitously arriving in a prowl car, and getting out, and coming over to where the woman is babbling and the patrolman is listening with a puzzled expression on his face.

The person who hit her is her husband, the woman says. But she does not want to press charges. That's not what she wants from the police.

The sergeant knows an assault when he sees one and is not particularly interested in whether or not the woman wants to press charges. But it is a nice Sunday night in April, and he would much rather stand here on the sidewalk and listen to the woman (who is not bad-looking, and who is wearing a nylon wrapper over nothing but bikini panties) than go upstairs to arrest whoever clobbered her over the eye.

The woman is upset because her husband has said he is going to kill himself. He hit her over the eye with a milk bottle and then he locked himself in the bathroom and started running the water in the tub and yelling that he was going to kill himself. The woman does not want him to kill himself because she loves him. That's why she ran down into the street, practically naked, to find the nearest cop. So he could stop her husband from killing himself.

The sergeant is somewhat bored. He keeps assuring the woman that anybody who's going to kill himself doesn't go around advertising it, he just goes right ahead and *does* it. But the woman is hysterical and still bleeding, and the sergeant feels he ought to set a proper example for the young patrolman. "Come on, kid," he says, and the two of them start into the tenement building while the patrolman at the wheel of the r.m.p. car radios in for a meat wagon. The lady sits weakly on the fender of the car. She has just begun to notice that she is pouring blood from the open cut over her eye, and has gone very pale. The patrolman at the wheel thinks she is going to faint, but he does not get out of the car.

On the third floor of the building (Apartment 31, the lady told them), the sergeant knocks briskly on the closed door, waits, listens, knocks again, and then turns to the patrolman and again says, "Come on, kid." The door is unlocked. The apartment is still save for the sound of running water in the bathroom.

"Anybody home?" the sergeant calls. There is no answer. He shrugs, makes a "Come on, kid" gesture with his head, and starts for the closed bathroom door. He is reaching for the knob when the door opens.

The man is naked.

He has climbed out of the tub where the water still runs, and his pale white body is glistening wet. The water in the tub behind him is red. He has slashed the arteries of his left wrist, and he is gushing blood onto the white tile floor while behind him water splashes into the tub. He holds a broken milk bottle in his right hand, presumably the same bottle with which be struck his wife, and the moment he throws open the bathroom door he swings the bottle at the sergeant's head. The sergeant is concerned about several things, and only one of them has to do with the possibility that he may be killed in the next few moments. He is concerned about grappling with a naked man, he is concerned about getting blood on his new uniform, he is concerned about putting on a good show for the patrolman.

The man is screaming, "Leave me alone, let me die," and lunging repeatedly at the sergeant with the jagged ends of the broken bottle. The sergeant, fat and puffing, is trying desperately to avoid each new lunge, trying to grab the man's arm, trying to stay out of the way of those pointed glass shards, trying to draw his revolver, trying to do all these things while the man keeps screaming and thrashing and thrusting the bottle at his face and neck.

There is a sudden shocking explosion. The bleeding man lets out a final scream and drops the bottle. It shatters on the tile, and the sergeant watches in bug-eyed fascination as the man keels over backwards and falls into the redstained water in the tub. The sergeant wipes sweat from his lip and turns to look at the patrolman, whose smoking service revolver is in his hand. The patrolman's eyes are squinched in pain. He keeps staring at the tub where the man has sunk beneath the surface of the red water.

"Nice going, kid," the sergeant says.

• • •

The city is asleep.

The street lamps are all that glow now, casting pale illumination over miles and miles of deserted sidewalks. In the apartment buildings the windows are dark save for an occasional bathroom, where a light flickers briefly and then dies. Everything is still. So still.

Take a look at this city.

How can you possibly hate her?

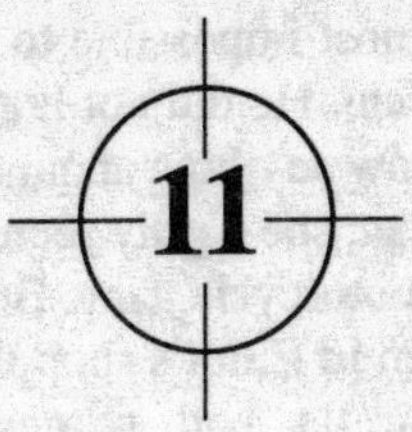

He had been searching for Mary Margaret Ryan without success since Saturday afternoon. He had tried the apartment on Porter Street, where she said she was living, but Henry and Bob told him she hadn't been around, and they had no idea where she was. He had then tried all the neighborhood places she might have frequented, and had even staked out Elliot's shop, on the off chance she might go there to see him. But she had not put in an appearance.

Now, at ten o'clock on Monday morning, April 26, four days before the Deaf Man had promised to steal $500,000 from the First Federal Bank (though God knew which one), Carella roamed Rutland Street looking for a silver motorcycle. During their brief conversation last Tuesday, Yank had told Carella that he'd blown in a few weeks back and was living in an apartment on Rutland. He had not given the address, but

Carella didn't think he'd have too much trouble finding the place—it is almost impossible to hide something as large as a motorcycle. He did not honestly expect Yank or his friends to know anything about the whereabouts of Mary Margaret Ryan; she hardly seemed the kind of girl who'd run with a motorcycle gang. But Yank and a bikie named Ox had been in Elliot's shop the day before, and the argument Carella had witnessed through the plate-glass window seemed something more than casual. When you run out of places to look, you'll look anywhere. Mary Margaret Ryan had to be someplace; *everybody's* got to be someplace, man.

After fifteen minutes on the block, he located *three* bikes chained to the metal post of a banister in the downstairs hallway of 601 Rutland. He knocked on the door of the sole apartment on the ground floor, and asked the man who answered it where the bikies were living.

"You going to bust them?" the man asked.

"What apartment are they in?"

"Second-floor front," the man said. "I wish you'd clean them out of here."

"Why?"

"Because they're no damn good," the man said, and closed the door.

Carella went up to the second floor. Several brown bags of garbage were leaning against the wall. He listened outside the door, heard voices inside, and knocked. A blond man, naked to the waist, opened the door. He was powerful and huge, with hard, tight muscles developed by years of weight-lifting. Barefooted, with blue jeans stretched tight over bulging thighs, he looked out at Carella and said nothing.

"Police officer," Carella said. "I'm looking for some people named Ox and Yank."

"Why?" the blonde said.

"Couple of questions I want to ask them."

The blonde studied him, shrugged, said, "Okay," and led him into the apartment. Ox and Yank were sitting at a table in the kitchen, drinking beer.

"Well, well," Yank said.

"Who's this?" Ox asked.

"A gentleman from the police," Yank said, and added with mock formality, "I fear I've forgotten your name, officer."

"Detective Carella."

"Carella, Carella, right. What can we do for you, Detective Carella?"

"Have you seen Mary Margaret around?" Carella asked.

"Who?"

"Mary Margaret Ryan."

"Don't know her," Yank said.

"How about you?" Carella said.

"Nope," Ox answered.

"Me, neither," the blonde said.

"Girl about this high," Carella said, "long brown hair, brown eyes."

"Nope," Yank said.

"Reason I ask . . ."

"We don't know her," Yank said.

"Reason I ask," Carella repeated, "is that she poses for Sanford Elliot, and . . ."

"Don't know him, either," Yank said.

"You don't, huh?"

"Nope."

"None of you know him, huh?"

"None of us," Yank said.

"Have you had any second thoughts about that picture I showed you?"

"Nope, no second thoughts," Yank said. "Sorry."

"You want to take a look at this picture, Ox?"

"What picture?" Ox asked.

"This one," Carella said, and took the photograph from his notebook.

He handed it to Ox, looking into his face, looking into his eyes, and becoming suddenly unsettled by what he saw there. Through the plate-glass window of Elliot's shop, Ox had somehow appeared both intelligent and articulate, perhaps because he had been delivering a finger-waving harangue. But now, after having heard his voice, after having seen his eyes, Carella knew at once that he was dealing with someone only slightly more alert than a beast of the field. The discovery was frightening. Give me the smart ones anytime, Carella thought. I'll take a thousand like the Deaf Man if you'll only keep the stupid ones away from me.

"Recognize him?" he asked.

"No," Ox said, and tossed the photograph onto the table.

"I was talking to Sanford Elliot Saturday," Carella said. "I thought *he* might be able to help me with this picture." He picked it up, put it back into his notebook, and waited. Neither Ox nor Yank said a word. "You say you don't know him, huh?"

"*What* was the name?" Ox said.

"Sanford Elliot. His friends call him Sandy."

"Never heard of him," Ox said.

"Uh-huh," Carella said. He looked around the room. "Nice place, is it yours?" he asked the bare-chested, barefooted blond man.

"Yeah."

"What's your name?"

"Who says I have to tell you?"

"That garbage stacked in the hallway is a violation," Carella said flatly. "You want me to get snotty, or you want to tell me your name?"

"Willie Harcourt."

"How long have you been living here, Willie?"

"About a year."

"When did your friends arrive?"

"I told you . . ." Yank started.

"I'm asking your pal. When did they get here, Willie?"

"Few weeks ago."

Carella turned to Ox and said, "What's your beef with Sandy Elliot?"

"What?" Ox said.

"Sandy Elliot."

"We told you we don't know him," Yank said.

"You've got a habit of answering questions nobody asked you," Carella said. "I'm talking to your friend here. What's the beef, Ox? You want to tell me?"

"No beef," Ox said.

"Then why were you yelling at him?"

"Me? You're crazy."

"You were in his shop Saturday, and you were yelling at him. Why?"

"You must have me mixed up with somebody else," Ox said, and lifted his beer bottle and drank.

"Who else lives in this apartment?" Carella asked.

"Just the three of us," Willie said.

"Those your bikes downstairs?"

"Yes," Yank said quickly.

"Pal," Carella said, "I'm going to tell you one last time . . ."

"Yeah, *what* are you going to tell me?" Yank asked, and rose from the table and put his hands on his hips.

"You're a big boy, I'm impressed," Carella said, and, without another word, drew his gun. "This is a .38 Detective's Special," he said. "It carries six cartridges, and I'm a great shot. I don't intend tangling with three gorillas. Sit down and be nice, or I'll shoot you in the foot and say you were attempting to assault a police officer."

Yank blinked.

"Hurry up," Carella said.

Yank hesitated only a moment longer, and then sat at the table again.

"Very nice," Carella said. He did not holster the pistol. He kept it in his hand, with his finger inside the trigger guard. "The silver bike is yours, isn't it?" he asked.

"Yeah."

"Which one is yours, Ox?"

"The black."

"How about you?" he said, turning to Willie.

"The red one."

"They all properly registered?"

"Come on," Yank said, "you're not going to hang any bullshit violation on us."

"Unless I decide to lean on you about the garbage outside."

"Why you doing this?" Ox asked suddenly.

"Doing what, Ox?"

"Hassling us this way? What the hell did we do?"

"You lied about being in Elliot's shop Saturday, that's what you did."

"Big deal. Okay, we were there. So what?"

"What were you arguing about?"

"The price of a statue," Ox said.

"It didn't look that way."

"That's all it was," Ox said. "We were arguing about a price."

"What'd you decide?"

"Huh?"

"What price did you agree on?"

"We didn't."

"How well do you know Elliot?"

"Don't know him at all. We saw his stuff in the window, and we went in to ask about it."

"What about Mary Margaret Ryan?"

"Never heard of her."

"Okay," Carella said. He went to the door, opened it, and said, "If you were planning to leave suddenly for the Coast, I'd advise against it. I'd also advise you to get that garbage out of the hallway." He opened the door, stepped outside, closed the door behind him, and went down the steps. He did not return the gun to its holster until he was on the ground floor again. He knocked on the door at the end of the hall there, and the same man answered it.

"Did you bust them?" the man asked.

"No. Mind if I come in a minute?"

"You should have busted them," the man said, but he stepped aside and allowed Carella to enter the apartment. He was a man in his fifties, wearing dark trousers, house slippers, and an undershirt with shoulder straps. "I'm the superintendent here," he said.

"What's your name, sir?" Carella asked.

"Andrew Halloran," the super said. "And yours?"

"Detective Carella."

"Why didn't you bust them, Detective Carella? They give me a hell of a lot of trouble, I wish you would have busted them for something."

"Who's paying for the apartment, Mr. Halloran?"

"The one with all the muscles. His name's William Harcourt. They call him Willie. But he's never there alone. They come and go all the time. Sometimes a dozen of them are living in there at the same time, men and women, makes no difference. They get drunk, they take dope, they yell, they fight with each other and with anybody tries to say a decent word to them. They're no damn good, is all."

"Would you know the full names of the other two?"

"Which two is that?" Halloran asked.

"Ox and Yank."

"I get mixed up," Halloran said. "Three of them came in from California a few weeks back, and I sometimes have trouble telling them apart. I think the two up there with Willie . . ."

"*Three* of them, did you say?" Carella asked, and suddenly remembered that Yank had given him this same information last Tuesday, when he'd been sitting outside the candy store with his chair tilted back against the brick wall. *"Three of us blew in from the Coast a few weeks back."*

"Yeah, three of them, all right. Raising all kinds of hell, too."

"Can you describe them to me?"

"Sure. One of them's short and squat, built like an ape with the mind of one besides."

"That'd be Ox."

"Second one's got frizzy hair and a thick black beard, scar over his right eye."

"Yank. And the third one?"

"Tall fellow with dark hair and a handlebar mustache.

Nicest of the lot, matter of fact. I haven't seen him around for a while. Not since last week sometime. I don't think he's left for good, though, because his bike's still here in the hall."

"Which bike?"

"The red one."

"I thought that belonged to Willie."

"Willie? Hell, he's lucky if he can afford roller skates."

Carella took the notebook from his jacket pocket, removed the photograph from it, and asked, "Is this the third bikie?"

"That's Adam, all right," Halloran said.

"Adam *what*?" Carella said.

"Adam Villers."

He called the squadroom from a pay phone in the corner drugstore, told Meyer he'd had a positive identification of the dead boy in the Jesus Case, and asked him to run a routine I.S. check on Adam Villers, V-I-L-L-E-R-S. He then asked if there had been any calls for him.

"Yeah," Meyer said. "Your sister called and said not to forget Wednesday is your father's birthday and to mail him a card."

"Right. Anything else?"

"Kling wants to know if you feel like taking your wife to a strip joint in Calm's Point."

"What?"

"He's tailing a guy on those burglaries, and the guy knows what he looks like, and Cotton was spotted for a cop first crack out of the box."

"Tell Kling I've got nothing better to do right now than take Teddy to a strip joint in Calm's Point. Jesus!"

"Don't get sore at *me*, Steve."

"Any other calls?"

"Did you have a mugging on Ainsley back in March? Woman named Charity Miles?"

"Yes."

"The Eight-eight just cracked it. Guy's admitted to every crime of the past century, including the Brink's Robbery."

"Good, that's one less to worry about. Anything else?"

"Nothing."

"Any mail?"

"Another picture from our Secret Pen Pal."

"Who'd he send this time?"

"Who do you think?" Meyer said.

He did not find Mary Margaret Ryan until close to midnight. It had begun drizzling lightly at 11:45 P.M., by which time he had tried the apartment on Porter again, as well as all the neighborhood hangouts, and was ready to give up and go home. He recognized her coming out of a doorway on Hager. She was wearing an army poncho, World War II salvage stuff, camouflaged for jungle warfare. She walked swiftly and purposefully, and he figured she was heading back for the apartment, not two blocks away. He caught up with her on the corner of Hager and McKay.

"Mary Margaret," he said, and she turned abruptly, her eyes as wide and frightened as they had been that first day he'd talked to her.

"What do you want?" she said.

"Where are you going?" he asked.

"Home," she said. "Excuse me, I . . ."

"Few things I'd like to ask you."

"No," she said, and began walking up McKay.

He caught her elbow and turned her to face him, and looked down into her eyes and said, "What are you afraid of, Mary Margaret?"

"Nothing, leave me alone. I have to get home."

"Why?"

"Because . . . I'm packing. I'm getting out of here. Look," she said, plaintively, "I finally got the money I need, and I'm splitting, so leave me alone, okay? Let me just get the fuck *out* of here."

"Why?"

"I've had this city."

"Where are you going?"

"To Denver. I hear the scene's good there. *Anything's* better than here."

"Who gave you the money?"

"A girlfriend. She's a waitress at the Yellow Bagel. She makes good money. It's only a loan, I'll pay her back. Look, I got to catch a plane, okay? I got to go now. I don't like it here. I don't like anything *about* this city. I don't like the look of it, I don't like the people, I don't like . . ."

"Where've you been hiding?"

"I *haven't* been hiding. I was busy trying to raise some bread, that's all. I had to talk to a lot of people."

"You were *hiding*, Mary Margaret. Who from?"

"Nobody."

"Who the hell are you *running* from?"

"Nobody, nobody."

"What was Sandy doing in that abandoned building on the eighteenth?"

"I don't know what you mean."

"Were *you* there, too?"

"No."

"*Where* were you?"

"I told you. In Boston. We were both in Boston."

"*Where* in Boston?"

"I don't know."

"How'd Sandy burn his foot?"

"Burn? It's not burned, it's . . ."

"It's *burned.* How'd it happen?"

"I don't know. Please, I have to . . ."

"Who killed Adam Villers?"

"Adam? How . . . how do you . . . ?"

"I know his name, and I know when he got here, and

I know his friends have been to see Sandy. Now how about it, Mary Margaret?"

"Please, please . . ."

"Are you going to tell me what happened, or . . . ?"

"Oh my God, oh my God," she said, and suddenly covered her face with her hands and began sobbing. They stood in the rain, Mary Margaret weeping into her hands, Carella watching her for only a moment before he said, "You'd better come with me."

The three of them had only arrived a few days before, and still hadn't caught up with their friend, the blond one with the muscles, I don't know his name. So they were flopping in the building on Harrison when they first made contact with Sandy. It was Adam Villers who came into the shop. He was a decent person, Adam. There's nothing that says bikies can't be decent. He was honestly trying to set something up. And it cost him his life.

What he did was he came into the shop to tell Sandy how much he liked his work. He's a good artist, you know, a really good one, well, you saw his stuff, you know how good he is. But he just wasn't *selling* much, and it costs a lot to cast those things in bronze, and he was running low on bread, which is why Adam's idea sounded like such a good one. Adam said the guys he ran with could pack the stuff in their bike bags, and try to sell it, you know, like wherever they traveled. He said they couldn't pay what Sandy was asking in the shop, but they'd take a *lot* of it, you see, and he could make it up in volume. So Sandy agreed to go up there—to where they were living on Harrison—and talk price with them, to see if it would be worth it to him. Adam really thought . . . I mean, Adam had no idea what the other two were after. You read a lot about bikies, and you get all these ideas about them, but Adam was okay. He really dug the work Sandy was doing, and figured we could all make a little money out of it. That's why he took us there that night.

They were living in two rooms on the fifth floor. One of the rooms had a mattress in it. In the other room, they had built a small fire in the center of the floor. The one called Yank was trying to fix something from his bike when we came in. I don't know what it was, something that had fallen off his bike. He was trying to hammer a dent out of it. Anyway, we all sat around the fire, and Sandy offered them some grass, and we smoked a little while Adam explained his idea about buying Sandy's work at discount and selling it on the road, which he figured would pay for all their traveling expenses. The one called Ox said that he had looked over the stuff in the shop window the other day and thought the girl was very sexy.

I think that was when I first began to get scared.

But . . . anyway, we . . . we went on talking about how much the sculpture was worth. Adam was still very excited about the whole thing, and trying to figure out how much Sandy should get for pieces that were this big or that big, you know, trying to work out a legitimate business deal. I mean, that's why we'd gone up there. Because it looked like a good way to make a little bread. So all of a sudden Ox said How much do you want for the girl?

We were all, I guess, I mean, surprised, you know? Because it came out of the blue, like, when we were talking about Sandy's work and all, and we just sat there sort of stunned and Ox said You hear me? How much you want for the girl?

What girl? Sandy said.

This one, Ox said, and reached over and . . . and poked my breast, poked his finger at my breast.

Hey, come on, Adam said, knock it off, Ox, we're here to talk about the guy's work, okay?

And Ox said I'd rather talk about the guy's girl.

Sandy got up and said Come on, Mary Margaret, let's get out of here, and that was when Ox hit him and it all started. I screamed, I guess, and Ox hit me, too, hard, he punched me in the ribs, it still hurts where he hit me. They . . . Adam started to yell at them, and Yank grabbed him from behind and held his arms while Ox . . . Ox dragged Sandy over to the fire and pulled off his sneaker and stuck his foot in the flames, and told him next time they asked a question about the price of something he should answer nice instead of being such a wise guy. Sandy passed out, and I began screaming again because . . . Sandy was . . . his foot was all black and . . . and Ox hit me again and threw me on the floor and that was when Adam broke away from Yank, to try to help me. They both turned on him. Like animals. Like sharks. Like attacking their own, do you know? In frenzy, do you know? They went after him, they chased him down the hallway, they . . . I heard sounds like . . . hammering, I knew later it was hammering, and I heard Adam screaming, and I ran down the hall and saw what they had done and fainted. I don't know what they did to me while I was unconscious. I was . . . I was bleeding bad when I woke up . . . but they were gone, thank God, they were gone at last.

I didn't know what to do. Sandy could hardly walk and there . . . there was a dead man down the hall, Adam was dead down the hall. I . . . put Sandy's arm over my shoulder, and we started down the steps, all I could think of was getting away from there. Have you seen that place? The steps are covered with all kinds of crap, it's like walking through a junkyard. But I got him down to the street, he was in such pain, oh God, he kept moaning, and we couldn't find a taxi, there are never any taxis in this neighborhood. But finally we got one, and I took him over to the clinic at Buenavista Hospital, and they treated his foot, and we hoped it was all over, we hoped we'd seen the last of them.

They came back to the shop the next day. They said we'd better keep our mouths shut about what happened or the same thing would happen to us. We made up the story about Boston, we knew the police might get to us, we figured we needed an alibi. And . . . we've been waiting for them to leave, praying they'd go back to California, leave us alone, get out of our lives.

Now they'll kill us, won't they?

He was not foolish enough to go after them alone. The three bikes were still chained to the metal hall banister, silver, red, and black. He and Meyer went past them swiftly and silently, guns drawn, and climbed to the second floor. They fanned out on both sides of the door to Apartment 2A and then, facing each other, put their ears to the door and listened.

"How many?" Carella whispered.

"I can make out at least four," Meyer whispered back.

"You ready?"

"Ready as I'll ever be."

The worst part about kicking in a door is that you never know what might be on the other side of it. You can listen for an hour, you can distinguish two different voices, or five, or eight, and then break in to find an army with sawed-off shotguns, determined to blow you down the stairs and out into the gutter. Meyer had heard four distinctly different voices, which was exactly what Carella thought he had heard. They were all men's voices, and he thought he recognized two of them as belonging to Ox and Yank. He did not think the bikies would be armed, but he had no way of knowing whether his supposition was true or not. There was nothing to do but go in after them. There was nothing to do but take them.

Carella nodded at Meyer, and Meyer returned the nod.

Backing across the hall, gun clutched in his right hand, Carella braced himself against the opposite wall, and then shoved himself off it, right knee coming up, and hit the door with a hard flat-footed kick just below the lock. The door sprang inwards, followed by Carella at a run, Meyer behind him and to the left. Ox and Willie were sitting at the kitchen table, drinking wine. Yank was standing near the refrigerator, talking to a muscular black man.

Ox threw back his chair, and a switchblade knife snapped open in his hand. He was coming at Carella with the knife clutched tight in his fist when Carella fired. The first slug had no effect on him. Like a rampaging elephant, he continued his charge, and Carella fired again, and then once more, and still Ox came, finally hurling himself onto Carella, the knife blade grazing his face and neck as he pulled off another shot, the muzzle of the gun pushed hard into Ox's belly. There was a muffled explosion. The slug knocked Ox backward onto the kitchen table. He twisted over onto his side, bubbling blood, and then rolled to the floor.

Nobody was moving.

Yank, at the refrigerator with the muscular black man, seemed ready to make a break. The look was in his eyes, the trapped look of a man who knows it's all over, there's nothing to lose, stay or run, there's nothing to lose. Meyer recognized the look because he had seen it a hundred times before. He did not know who any of these men were, but he knew that Yank was the one about to break, and was therefore extremely dangerous.

He swung the gun on him.

"Don't," he said.

That's all he said.

The gun was steady in his hand, leveled at Yank's heart. A new look came into Yank's eyes, replacing the trapped and desperate glitter that had been in them not a moment before. Meyer had seen this look, too; there was nothing new under the sun. It was a look composed of guilt, surrender, and relief. He knew now that Yank would stay right where he was until the cuffs were closed on his wrists. There would be no further trouble.

Willie Harcourt sat at the kitchen table with his eyes wide in terror. Ox was at his feet, dead and bleeding, and Willie had urinated in his pants when the shooting began. He was afraid to move now because he thought they might shoot him, too; he was also ashamed to move because if he did they would see he had wet himself.

"Is there a phone in here?" Carella asked.

"N-n-no," Willie stammered.

"What's *your* name, mister?" Carella asked the black man.

"Frankie Childs. I don't know these guys from a hole in the wall. I came up for a little wine, that's all."

"You're bleeding, Steve," Meyer said.

Carella touched his handkerchief to his face.

"Yeah," he said, and tried to catch his breath.

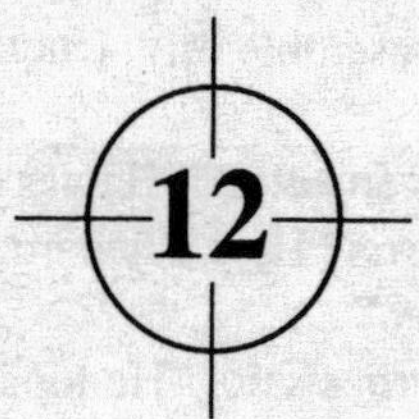

The boys were beginning to enjoy themselves.

After all, if there had to be bank robberies (and in their line of work, there most certainly had to be bank robberies), they preferred dealing with a criminal who at least *tried* to make it all a little more interesting. For where indeed was there any joy in coping with some jerk whose idea of a brilliant holdup was to walk in and stick a gun in a person's face? The boys had to admit it—the Deaf Man brought a spot of needed cheer to that dingy old squadroom.

"Who do you suppose it is?" Byrnes asked.

Hawes looked at the photostat, which had arrived in Tuesday morning's mail, and then said, "He looks a lot like Meyer."

"Except Meyer hasn't got as much hair."

"I fail to see the humor," Meyer said, and then

studied the picture more carefully. "Now that you mention it, he does resemble my Uncle Morris in New Jersey."

"You think he's an actor?" Hawes asked.

"My Uncle Morris? He's a haberdasher."

"I mean this guy."

"I doubt it," Byrnes said. "He looks too intelligent."

"He might be an actor, though," Meyer said. "Somebody out of *Great Expectations.*"

"He does look English."

"Or *Bleak House*," Meyer said.

"He looks like an English lawyer," Hawes said.

"Maybe he's Charles Dickens himself," Meyer said.

"Maybe. English lawyers and English writers all look alike."

"Maybe he's a famous English murderer."

"Or a famous English sex fiend."

"*All* the English are famous sex fiends."

"He *does* look very sexy," Byrnes said.

"It's the hair. It's the way he's got the hair teased."

"I like his tie, too."

"His cravat."

"Yes, but also his tie."

"Who the hell is he?" Byrnes asked.

"Who the hell knows?" Meyer said.

The Deaf Man held out the slate and asked "Do you understand all of it so far?"

"Yes," Harold said. "I go into the vault with the bank manager . . ."

"His name is Alton."

"Right. I clean out the place, and then take him back

to the office."

"Meanwhile," Roger said, "Danny and me are in the car, right outside the teller's window."

"And you, Florence?"

"I'm in my stalled car at the head of the driveway."

"In the manager's office," Harold said, "I clobber him and tie him up."

"I'm out of the car by then," Danny said, "busting the window."

"I run out of the manager's office, go through the gate, and jump out the broken window."

"I help him climb through."

"We both get in the car . . ."

"I step on the gas," Roger said.

"I pick you up, Mr. Taubman, at the front of the bank," Florence said.

"And we're off and running."

"Perfect," the Deaf Man said. "Any questions?"

"Do we come straight back here, or what?"

"No. I've already reserved rooms for all of us at the Allister."

"Why there?"

"Why not?"

"Why not right here at the Remington?"

"This is a flea bag. I chose it for our meetings only because it's inconspicuous."

"That's just my point. The Allister's right in the middle of everything."

"Exactly. You, Roger, and Danny are three respectable businessmen checking into one of the biggest hotels in the city. Florence and I are man and wife arriving from Los Angeles. We'll meet in Roger's room at three o'clock, and share the money at that time. On Saturday morning, we'll all check out and go our separate ways."

"Five hundred thousand bucks," Harold said, and whistled softly.

"Give or take a few thousand," the Deaf Man said. "Any other questions?"

"The only part that bothers me is the double cross," Roger said.

"Let *me* worry about that," the Deaf Man said. "All you have to worry about is doing your part. I rather imagine a hundred thousand dollars will ease your conscience considerably."

"Still . . ."

"I don't want second thoughts about this, Roger. If you're not with us, say so now. We won't be going through the dry run until Thursday, and I won't reveal the location of the bank until then. You're free to go. Just have the decency to do it now, while I can still find a replacement."

"I guess I'm in," Roger said.

"No guesswork, Roger. Yes or no?"

"Yes."

"Good. Does the duplicity bother anyone else?"

"I only worry about number one," Danny said.

"I never met a man I could trust," Florence said, "and I don't expect nobody to trust me, either."

"How about you, Harold?"

"I want that hundred thousand dollars," Harold said simply.

"Then I take it we're all committed," the Deaf Man said.

• • •

Patrolman Mike Ingersoll came into the squadroom at four o'clock that afternoon. He had been relieved on post fifteen minutes ago, and had already changed into street attire—brown trousers and tan sports shirt, a poplin, zippered jacket. Kling was sitting at his desk with Mrs. Ungerman, showing her mug shots in the hope she might be able to identify the man with whom she had briefly waltzed last Thursday night. He motioned to Ingersoll to come in, and Ingersoll motioned back that if Kling was busy, and Kling motioned back, No, that's okay—and all the pantomime caused Mrs. Ungerman to turn curiously toward the railing.

"Hello, Mrs. Ungerman," Ingersoll said, and smiled pleasantly.

Mrs. Ungerman looked at him in puzzlement.

"Patrolman Ingersoll," he said.

"Oh," she said. "Oh, of course. I didn't recognize you without the uniform."

"I'll just be a minute, Mike," Kling said.

"Sure, sure, take your time," Ingersoll said, and wandered over to the bulletin board and studied the Deaf Man's art gallery. He knew nothing about the case, and thought the photostats were some kind of little joke the detectives were playing up here in the rarefied atmosphere on the second floor of the building. At Kling's desk Mrs. Ungerman kept looking at photographs of known burglars and shaking her head. At last she rose, and Kling thanked her for her time. She waved at Ingersoll, said, "Nice seeing you," and went out of the squadroom.

"Any help?" Ingersoll said, coming over to the desk.

"None at all."

Ingersoll pulled up a chair and sat. "Have you got a minute?" he asked.

"Don't tell me we've had another burglary."

"No, no," Ingersoll said, and knocked the desk with his knuckles. "Been very quiet this week, thank God. This is what I want to talk to you about." Ingersoll paused, and then shifted his weight and leaned closer to Kling, lowering his voice, as if he did not want his words to be overheard even within the sanctified walls of a detective squadroom. "How would you like to set a trap for our heist artist?" he said.

"Stick a man in one of the empty apartments, you mean?"

"Yeah."

"I thought of that, Mike, but I'm not sure it'd work."

"Why not?"

"If these are inside jobs, the guy's probably watching all the time, don't you think? He'll know we've got a stakeout going."

"Maybe not. Besides, we're up a dead-end street right now. Anything's worth a chance."

"Well, I've got a lead, you know. Let's see what happens there before we go spending the night . . ."

"What kind of lead, Bert?" Ingersoll said, and took out his notebook. "Anything I should know?"

"The guy dropped a ballpoint pen in the Blair apartment."

"Pretty girl," Ingersoll said.

"Yeah," Kling said, and hoped he sounded noncommittal. "Anyway, I tracked it to an ex-con named Fred Lipton, two previous convictions."

"For Burglary?"

"No, Dis Cond and Forgery One."

"He live around here?"

"Calm's Point."

"Whereabouts? *I* live in Calm's Point, you know."

"He works for a real estate agency on Ashmead Avenue, and lives in a garden apartment on Ninety-eighth and Aurora."

"That's not too far from me," Ingersoll said. "Anything I can do for you out there?"

"You look too much like a cop," Kling said, and smiled.

"What do you mean?"

"Lipton's friendly with a dancer at a joint called the Gee-Gee-Go-Go."

"Yeah, I know the place, it's a real dive."

"Hawes tried to pump the girl the other night, but she made him for a cop right off."

"Well, he *does* look kind of like a cop," Ingersoll said, and nodded. "You sure you don't want me to take a whack at it?"

"I thought I'd ask Willis."

"Yeah, he'd be perfect," Ingersoll said. "But meanwhile, can't we set something up right here? In case you *don't* get anything on Lipton?"

"I really think it'd be a waste of time, Mike."

"The Ungerman hit was the last one, am I right? That was five days ago, Bert. It's not like this guy to stay inactive for such a long time."

"Maybe he's cooling it because the old lady got a look at him."

"What's that got to do with it? He wouldn't go back to the same apartment twice, would he?"

"No, that's right."

"The way I figure it, Bert, he's trying to knock off as

many places as he can while people are still taking winter vacations."

"I don't get you, Mike."

"Look at the M.O., Bert. A dozen places in February and March, and three more in the last . . . how long has it been? Two weeks?"

"About that, yeah."

"Okay, this is still April, people are still going away a little. We get into May and June, most of them'll be staying home. Until the summer months, you know? So he hasn't got much time before he has to lay off. And he *missed* on the Ungerman job, don't forget that. I figure he's got to be coming out again real soon."

"So what's your idea?"

"I've been talking to some of the supers in the neighborhood, there are maybe three or four apartments with people away. I figure we can stake out at least two of them every night, more if the Loot'll let you have additional men. We rotate the apartments, we stay in touch with walkie-talkies, and we take our chances. What do you think?"

"I don't think the Loot'll give me any men."

"How about Captain Frick? You think I should ask him?"

"I wouldn't, Mike. If you want to try this just the two of us, I'm game. But I can guarantee we won't get any help. Things are just too goddamn busy around here."

"Okay, so you want to do it?"

"When?"

"Tonight?"

"Okay, sure."

"Maybe we'll get lucky. If not, we'll try again tomorrow night. I don't go on the four-to-midnight till next week sometime, but even then I'm willing to stick with this till we get the son of a bitch."

"Well, we do have to sleep every now and then," Kling said, and smiled.

"We catch this guy, we can all take a rest," Ingersoll said, and returned the smile. "Look, Bert, I'll level with you. I'm anxious to grab him because it might help me get the gold tin. Even an assist might do it for me. I've been on the force twelve years now, been commended for bravery twice, and I'm still making a lousy eleven thousand a year. It's time I started helping myself, don't you think? I'm divorced, you know, did you know that?"

"No, I didn't."

"Sure. So I got alimony to pay, and also I'd like to get married again, I'm thinking about getting married again. There's a nice girl I want to marry. If we can crack this one together, it'd be a big help to me, Bert. I'm talking to you like a brother."

"I understand what you mean, Mike."

"You can understand how I feel, can't you?"

"Sure."

"So look, let me check out those apartments again, make sure the people didn't come back all of a sudden. I'll call in later and let you know where to meet me, okay?"

"Fine."

"You want to requisition the walkie-talkies, or shall I take care of it?"

"Why do we need walkie-talkies?"

"Well, the guy got careless on his last job. He may be armed this time, who knows? If we run into any kind of trouble, be nice to know we're in contact with each other."

"I'll get the walkie-talkies," Kling said.

"Good. I'll call you later."

"See you," Kling said, and watched Ingersoll go through the gate in the railing and down the corridor to the iron-runged stairway. He suddenly wondered why Ingersoll had set his promotion sights so low; the guy was *already* behaving like the goddamn commissioner.

Hal Willis was an experienced cop and a smart one. At the Gee-Gee-Go-Go that night he talked to Rhonda Spear for close to forty minutes, buying her six drinks during the course of their odd discussion. At the end of that time, he had elicited from her exactly nothing.

Willis did not look like a cop, and he was not carrying a gun, having been previously warned that Rhonda was quite adept at detecting the presence of hardware. Yet he was certain she had not given a single straight answer to any of his seemingly innocent questions. He could only assume that Hawes' abortive attempt to reach her had served as a warning against further conversation with any men who weren't regulars in the place. If you're not sure who's a cop and who isn't, it's best to behave as though *everyone* is. Especially if you've got something to hide. That was the one thing Willis came away with: the intuitive feeling that Rhonda Spear had a hell of a lot to hide.

Aside from that, the night was a total loss.

The night, for Kling and Ingersoll, was no more rewarding; it was merely longer. They sat in separate empty apartments three buildings away from each other, and waited for the burglar to strike. The walkie-talkie communication was sketchy at best, but they did manage to maintain contact with each other, and their infrequent conversations at least kept them awake. They did not leave the apartments until seven in the morning—no closer to solving the case than they had been at the start of the stakeout.

At ten minutes past two, shortly after the second mail had been delivered, the squadroom telephone rang, and Carella picked it up.

"87th Squad, Carella," he said.

"Good afternoon, Detective Carella."

He recognized the voice at once, and signaled for Meyer to pick up the extension.

"Good afternoon," he said. "Long time no hear."

"Has the mail arrived yet?" the Deaf Man asked.

"Few minutes ago."

"Have you opened it yet?"

"Not yet."

"Don't you think you should?"

"I have a feeling I already know what's in it."

"I may surprise you."

"No, I don't think so," Carella said. "The pattern's been pretty well established by now."

"Do you have the envelope there?"

"Yes, I have," Carella said, and separated the manila envelope from the rest of his mail. "By the way, it's Stephen with a *p–h*."

"Oh, forgive me," the Deaf Man said. "Open it, why don't you?"

"Will you hold on?"

"Surely," the Deaf Man said. "Not too long, though. We can't risk a trace, now can we?"

Carella tore open the flap, reached into the envelope, and pulled out the photostat:

"Big surprise," Carella said. "Who is this guy, anyway?"

"You mean you don't know?"

"We haven't been able to dope out any of it," Carella said.

"I think you're lying," the Deaf Man said, and hung up.

Carella waited. He knew the phone would ring again within the next few minutes, and he was not disappointed.

"87th Squad," he said, "Carella."

"Please forgive my precautionary measures," the Deaf Man said. "I'm not yet convinced of the effectiveness of telephone traces, but one can't be too careful these days."

"What's this picture gallery supposed to mean?" Carella said.

"Come, come, Carella, you're disappointing me."

"I'm serious. We think you've lost your marbles this time. Do you want to give us a hint or two?"

"Oh, I couldn't do that," the Deaf Man said. "I'm afraid you'll simply have to double your efforts."

"Not much time left, you know. Today's Wednesday, and you're pulling your big job on Friday, isn't that right?"

"Yes, that's absolutely true. Perhaps you ought to circle the date, Carella. So you won't forget it."

"I already have."

"Good. In that case, you're halfway home."

"What do you mean?"

"Think about it," the Deaf Man said, and again hung up.

Carella thought about it. He had a long time to think about it because the Deaf Man did not call again until three-thirty.

"What happened?" Carella asked. "Get involved in a big executive meeting?"

"I merely like to keep you off balance," the Deaf Man said.

"You do, you certainly do."

"What do you make of the most recent picture?"

"Have no idea who he is. Nor the woman, either. We recognized Hoover and Washington, of course . . . you're not planning a raid on the FBI, are you?"

"No, nothing as clever as that."

"We thought maybe you were going to fly to Washington in a Jap Zero and strafe . . ."

"Ah, then you *did* recognize the Zero?"

"Yes, we did. We're very well oriented up here."

"Please, no puns," the Deaf Man said, and Carella could swear he was wincing.

"But none of it makes any sense," Carella said. "Hoover, Washington, this guy with the mutton chops. What are you trying to tell us?"

"Does it really seem that difficult to you?"

"It certainly does."

"In that case, I'd merely accept the facts as they are, Carella."

"What facts?"

"The fact that you're incompetent . . ."

"Well, I wouldn't . . ."

"The fact that you're incapable of stopping me."

"Do you *want* us to stop you?"

"I'd like you to try."

"Why?"

"It's the nature of the beast, Carella. The delicate

symbiosis that keeps us both alive. You might call it a vicious circle," he said, and this time the word registered, this time Carella realized its use was deliberate. *Circle.*

"Might I call it that?" Carella said.

"I would strongly suggest it. Otherwise, you may merely come up with a zero," the Deaf Man said, and hung up.

Carella quickly put his own phone back onto the cradle, opened his top drawer, and removed from it the Isola telephone directory. The zero was a circle; the Deaf Man had just told him as much. And if he correctly recalled his cursory inspection of directory addresses . . .

He ran his finger swiftly down the page:

FIRST FEDERAL BANK
Main office 1265 Highland 380-1764
304 S 110 780-3751
60 Yates Av 271-0800
4404 Hrsy Blvd 983-6100
371 N 84 642-8751
14 VnBur Cir .231-7244

Carella went through the entire list in the Isola directory, and then checked all the First Federal addresses in the other four books as well. Only one of them seemed to fit. He buttoned the top button of his shirt, pulled up his tie, and was leaving the squadroom just as Meyer came back from the men's room down the hall.

"Where you off to?" Meyer asked.

"The library," Carella said.

• • •

That's who it was, all right.

The man with the fancy hair styling was none other than:

MARTIN VAN BUREN
1782-1862

EIGHTH PRESIDENT
OF
THE UNITED STATES
OF
AMERICA

In a city where streets, avenues, boulevards, bridges, airports, high schools, and even race tracks were named after past Presidents, it was perhaps no great honor to have a mere circle so-named—but then again, who remembered Van Buren except perhaps in Kinderhook, New York, where he'd been born? Anyway, there it was, Van Buren Circle. And at 14 Van Buren Circle, there was a branch of the First Federal Bank. At last it all made sense—or at least Carella *thought* it made sense. Which is exactly why he was suddenly so troubled. If everything made sense, then nothing made sense. Why would the Deaf Man pinpoint the exact location of a bank he planned to rob on a date he had already announced? Symbiosis aside, something else was surely coming, and Carella could not guess what.

An apartment is alive only when the people who live in it are there. When they are away, it becomes nothing more than a random collection of possessions, essentially lifeless. To a policeman sitting in the dark in the empty hours of the night, the place resembles a graveyard for furniture.

In the living room of 648 Richardson Drive that night, Bert Kling sat in an easy chair facing the front door, the walkie-talkie in his lap, his revolver in his right hand. It was difficult to stay awake. Occasionally, to relieve the monotony, he would contact Mike Ingersoll, who was in a similarly vacant apartment at 653 Richardson, across the street. Their conversations were almost as dreary as their separate vigils.

"Hello, Mike?"

"Yes, Bert."

"How's it going there?"

"Quiet."

"Same here."

"Talk to you later."

At ten minutes to midnight, the telephone rang. Sitting in the darkness, Kling nearly leaped out of the chair on the first ring, and then realized it was only the phone. He listened as it rang six times and then went silent. In as long as it took for the caller to re-dial, the phone began ringing again. This time there were fourteen rings before it went still. The caller might have been someone who did not know the tenants of the apartment were away; he had called once, assumed he'd misdialed, and tried again. On the other hand, the caller might have been the burglar, checking and then double-checking to make certain the tenants were *still* away. In which case, he now had his information and would come tiptoeing up to unlock the front door, let himself in, and burglarize to his heart's content.

Kling waited.

At twelve-thirty, Ingersoll contacted him on the walkie-talkie.

"Hello, Bert? Anything?"

"Telephone rang a while back, that's all."

"Nothing here, either."

"It's going to be a long night, Mike."

"No longer than last night," Ingersoll said.

"Talk to you."

"Right."

They talked to each other every forty minutes or so. Not one single burglar tried to enter either of the apartments all night long. At the first sign of light in the east, Kling contacted Ingersoll and suggested that they knock off. Ingersoll sighed and said, "Yeah, I guess so. You want some coffee before we head home?"

"Good idea," Kling said. "Meet you downstairs."

A patrol car was parked on the street in front of 657 Richardson, the building in which Augusta lived. Kling and Ingersoll walked to it rapidly. The patrolman behind the wheel recognized them and asked if they'd been sent over on the squeal.

"What squeal?" Kling asked.

"Guy ripped off an apartment in there."

"You're kidding," Kling said.

"Would I kid about a felony?" the patrolman asked, offended.

Kling and Ingersoll went into the building and knocked on the superintendent's door. It was answered by a woman in a bathrobe, who said her husband had gone upstairs to 6D, with the cop. Kling and Ingersoll took the elevator up, got out on the sixth floor, glanced down the hallway, and walked immediately to the left, where the partner of the patrolman in the car was examining a door and jamb for jimmy marks, the super standing just beside him.

"Anything?" Kling asked.

"No, it's clean, Bert," the patrolman said. "Guy must've got in with a key."

"Let's take a look, Mike," Kling said. To the patrolman, he said, "Have you called this in, Lew?"

"Henry took care of it downstairs. We knew what it was already 'cause the super'd been in here. In fact, I thought you was the detective they sent over."

"No," Kling said, and shook his head, and walked through the foyer into the apartment, Ingersoll directly behind him. The layout was identical to Augusta's apartment on the eleventh floor, and so he knew exactly where the bedroom was. The place was in total disorder, clothing strewn all over the room, drawers pulled from dressers and overturned.

"Something's missing," Ingersoll said.

"Huh?"

"No kitten."

They walked to the dresser. Kling, remembering Mr.

Angieri's experience, looked behind the dresser, thinking the kitten might have fallen there.

"Wait, here it is," Ingersoll said.

The kitten was a small glass figurine, white, with a blue bow around its neck. It sat next to a sterling-silver comb-and-brush set, which the burglar had apparently decided not to steal.

"Guess he's running out of live ones," Ingersoll said.

"Might get some prints from this, though," Kling said.

"I doubt it."

"Yeah, he's too smart for that."

"How do you like this son of a bitch?" Ingersoll said. "We're sitting in two apartments so close we could spit at him, and he's got the guts to rip off this joint. Jesus!"

"Let's talk to the super," Kling said.

The super's name was Phillip Trammel. He was a thin man in his sixties wearing bib overalls and a blue denim work shirt.

"How'd you discover the burglary?" Kling asked him.

"I was coming up to get the garbage. We ain't got no incinerator in this building. What the tenants do is they usually leave their garbage outside the service entrance in plastic bags, and I take it down to the basement for them. It's a little service we perform, you know? Ain't nothing says the super's supposed to go around picking up garbage, but I don't mind, it's a little extra service."

"So what happened?"

"I saw the door to 6D was open, and I knew we'd had

that burglary in Miss Blair's apartment little more'n a week ago, so I went inside and looked around. Somebody'd been in there, all right. So I called the police, and here you are."

"Here we are," Ingersoll said, and sighed.

When you are dealing with a man who sends you a picture of a football team, you have to believe he is crazy—unless you think you understand the way his mind works. The boys of the 87th would never in a million years have presumed to understand the workings of the Deaf Man's mind. But since they now possessed a considerable body of knowledge upon which to base some speculations, they turned to the latest photostat with something resembling scientific perspective.

If Washington meant First . . .

And Hoover meant Federal . . .

And Vilma Banky meant Bank . . .

What did a football team mean?

Van Buren, of course, meant only Van Buren, which was not much help.

But Zero meant Circle.

So what did a football team mean?

"Why not a baseball team?" Meyer asked.

"Or a hockey team," Carella said.

"Or a basketball, swimming, soccer, or lacrosse team," Hawes suggested.

"Why football?"

"What's he trying to tell us?"

"He's already told us all we need to know."

"Maybe he's just saying it's all a game to him."

"But why a *football* game?"

"Why not? A game's a game."

"Not to the Deaf Man."

"This isn't even the football season."

"Baseball's the game right now."

"So why football?"

"Anyway, he's already *told* us everything."

"That's what *I* said two minutes ago."

"Did somebody call the Eight-six?"

"I did. Yesterday afternoon."

"Will they be covering the bank tomorrow?"

"Like a dirty shirt."

"Maybe he's going to use eleven men on the job," Hawes said.

"What do you mean?"

"A football team. Eleven men."

"No, wait a second," Carella said. "What's the only thing he *hasn't* told us?"

"He's told it all. The date, the name of the bank, the address . . ."

"But not the *time.*"

"Eleven," Hawes said.

"Eleven o'clock," Meyer said.

"Yeah," Carella said, and reached for the phone. "Who's handling this at the Eight-six?"

The cops of the 86th Precinct were similar to the cops of the 87th Precinct, except that they had different names. Cops, like all other minority groups, are difficult to tell apart. Before Carella's call, Detective First-grade Albert Schmitt had already been in touch with Mr. Alton, the manager of the First Federal Bank. But now, supplied with new information about the anticipated holdup, he paid him another visit.

Mr. Alton, a portly little man with thinning white hair, was still visibly distressed over the first visit from the police. This new visit, pinpointing the *time* the bank would be robbed, contributed little toward soothing his dyspepsia.

"But I don't understand," he said. "Why would they be telling us exactly when they're coming?"

"Well, I don't quite know," Schmitt said thoughtfully. "Maybe they won't be coming at all, sir. Maybe this is just an elaborate hoax, who knows?"

"But you say this man has a record of . . ."

"Oh yes, he's given us trouble before. Not me personally, but the department. Which is why we're taking these precautions."

"I don't know," Mr. Alton said, shaking his head. "Friday is our busiest day. We cash checks for three payrolls on Friday. If you substitute . . ."

"Well, that's just what we think he's after, Mr. Alton. Those payrolls."

"Yes, but if you substitute your men for my tellers, how can we possibly serve our customers?"

"Would we be serving them better if we allowed this man to walk off with half a million dollars?"

"No, of course not, but . . ." Alton shook his head again. "What time will your men be here?"

"What time do you open?"

"Nine o'clock."

"That's what time we'll be here," Schmitt said.

In the squadroom of the 87th, perhaps because the boys felt they would soon be rid of the Deaf Man forever, they were telling deaf jokes.

"This man buys a hearing aid, you see," Meyer said, "and he's explaining to his friend how much he likes it. 'Best investment I ever made in my life,' he says. 'Before I put this thing in my ear, I was deaf as a post. Now, if I'm upstairs in the bedroom and the tea kettle goes off, I can hear it immediately. If a car pulls into the driveway, I can hear it when it's still a mile away. I'm telling you, this is the best investment I ever made.' His friend nods and asks, 'How much did it cost?' The guy looks at his watch and answers, 'A quarter to two.'"

The telephone rang.

Kling, laughing, picked it up and said, "87th Squad, Detective Kling."

"Bert, it's me."

"Oh, hi, Augusta."

"There's this guy," Hawes said, "who plays the violin beautifully. Whenever he plays the violin, people stop fighting, dogs and cats stop clawing at each other, he figures it's a real instrument for world peace."

"Bert, I'll be finished here in about a half hour," Augusta said. "How soon can you get away?"

"Not till four," Kling said. "Why?"

"I thought we might make love this afternoon."

"So he goes to the United Nations," Hawes said, "and they finance a test trip to the African jungle, figuring if he can play his violin for the wild animals there and make them stop fighting with each other, why then they'll finance a world-wide tour to promote peace."

"Well, uh," Kling said, and glanced at the other men, "I guess I can get away a little earlier. Where are you now?"

"I'm . . ."

"Just a second, let me find a pencil."

"In the middle of the jungle, he stops under a huge cork tree, takes out his violin, and begins playing," Hawes said.

"Go ahead," Kling said into the phone.

"The animals begin gathering around him—lions, rhinos, hippos, jackals, giraffes, all the animals of the jungle. This beautiful music is pouring from the violin, and the wild animals are all sitting around him in a circle, with their arms around each other, nobody fighting, everybody listening peacefully."

"Yes, I've got it," Kling said into the phone.

"But as the guy keeps playing," Hawes said, "a leopard creeps along a branch of the tree over his head, and suddenly leaps down at him, and eats him alive."

"See you in a half hour," Kling said, and hung up.

"The animals are appalled," Hawes said. "A lion steps out of the circle and says to the leopard, 'Why did you do that? This man came all the way from America to the wilds of the jungle here, and he brought his violin with him, and he played this beautiful music that made us all stop fighting. Why did you do such a terrible thing?' And the leopard cups his paw behind his ear and says, 'Huh?'"

Everyone burst out laughing except Kling.

"If Mike Ingersoll stops by," he said gruffly, like a detective investigating an important case, "I'll be at the Blair apartment."

In the dim silence of Augusta Blair's bedroom, they made love.

It was not so good.

"What's the matter?" Augusta whispered.

"I don't know," Kling whispered back.

"Am I doing something wrong?"

"No, no."

"Because if I am . . ."

"No, Augusta, really."

"Then what is it?"

"I think I'm a little afraid of you."

"Afraid?"

"Yes. I keep thinking, What's a dumb kid from Riverhead doing in bed with a beautiful model?"

"You're not a dumb kid," Augusta said, and smiled, and touched his mouth with her fingertips.

"I feel like a dumb kid."

"Why?"

"Because you're so beautiful."

"Bert, if you start that again, I'll hit you right on the head with a hammer."

"How'd you know about a hammer?"

"What?"

"A hammer. About it being the best weapon for a woman."

"I didn't know."

They were both silent for several moments.

"Relax," she said.

"I think that's exactly the problem," Kling said.

"If you want me to be ugly, I can be ugly as hell. Look," she said, and made a face. "How's that?"

"Beautiful."

"Where's my hammer?" she said, and got out of bed naked and padded out of the room. He heard her rummaging around in the kitchen. When she returned, she was indeed carrying a hammer. "Have you ever been hit with a hammer?" she asked, and sat beside him, pulling her long legs up onto the bed, crossing them Indian fashion, her head and back erect, the hammer clutched in her right hand.

"No," he said. "Lots of things, but never a hammer."

"Have you ever been shot?"

"Yes."

"Is that what this is?" she asked, and pointed with the hammer at the scar on his shoulder.

"Yes."

"Did it hurt?"

"Yes."

"Think I'll kiss it," she said, and bent over from the waist and kissed his shoulder lightly, and then sat up again. "You're dealing with the Mad Hammer Hitter here," she said. "One more word about how good-looking I am and, pow, your friends'll be investigating a homicide. You got that?"

"Got it," Kling said.

"This is the obligatory sex scene," she said. "I'm going to drive you to distraction in the next ten minutes. If you fail to respond, I'll cleave your skull with a swift single blow. In fact," she said, "a swift single blow might not be a bad way to start," and she bent over swiftly, her tongue darting. "I think you're beginning to get the message," she murmured. "Must be the goddamn hammer."

"Must be," Kling whispered.

Abruptly, she brought her head up to the pillow, stretched her legs, and rolled in tight against him, the hammer still in her right hand. "Listen, you," she whispered.

"I'm listening."

"We're going to be very important to each other."

"I know that."

"I'm scared to death," she said, and caught her breath. "I've never felt this way about any man. Do you believe me, Bert?"

"Yes."

"We're going to make love now."

"Yes, Augusta."

"We're going to make beautiful love."

"Yes."

"Yes, touch me," she said, and the hammer slipped from her grasp.

The telephone rang four times while they were in bed together. Each time, Augusta's answering service picked it up on the first ring.

"Might be someone important," Kling whispered after the last call.

"No one's more important than you," she whispered back, and immediately got out of bed and went into the kitchen. When she returned, she was carrying a split of champagne.

"Ah, good," he said. "How'd you know I was thirsty?"

"You open it while I think up a toast."

"You forgot glasses."

"Lovers don't need glasses."

"My grandmother does. Blind as a bat without them."

"Is she a lover?"

"Just ask Grandpa."

Kling popped the cork with his thumbs.

"Got that toast?" he asked.

"You're getting the bed wet."

"Come on, think of some people we can drink to."

"How about John and Martha Mitchell?"

"Why not? Here's to . . ."

"How about us?" Augusta said. She gently took the bottle from him, lifted it high, and said, "To Bert and Augusta. And to . . ." She hesitated.

"Yes?"

Solemnly, she studied his face, the bottle still extended. "And to at least the possibility of always," she said, and quickly, almost shyly, brought the bottle to her lips, drank from the open top, and handed it back to Kling. He did not take his eyes from her face. Watching her steadily, he said, "To us. And to always," and drank.

"Excuse me," Augusta said, and started out of the room.

"Leaving already, huh?" Kling said. "After all that sweet talk about . . ."

"I'm only going to the bathroom," Augusta said, and giggled.

"In that case, check the phone on the way back."

"Why?"

"I'm a cop."

"Hell with the phone," Augusta said.

But she nonetheless dialed her service, and then reported to Kling that the third call had been for him.

"Who was it?" he asked.

"A man named Meyer. He said Mrs. Ungerman is ready to make a positive identification."

• • •

Kling knocked on the door of Mike Ingersoll's Calm's Point apartment at ten minutes past eleven. He had heard voices inside, and now he heard footsteps approaching the door.

"Who's there?" Ingersoll asked.

"Me. Bert Kling."

"Who?"

"Kling."

"Oh. Oh, just a second, Bert."

Kling heard the night chain being slipped off, the lock turning. Ingersoll, wearing pajamas and slippers, opened the door wide, and said, "Hey, how are you? Come on in."

"I know it's late," Kling said. "You weren't asleep, were you?"

"No, no, I was just watching the news on television."

"Are you alone?"

"Yeah," Ingersoll said. "Come in, come in. Can I get you a beer?"

"No, Mike, thanks."

"Mind if I have one?"

"Go right ahead."

"Make yourself comfortable," Ingersoll said. "I'll be with you in a minute."

Kling went into the living room and sat in an easy chair facing the television set. Ingersoll's gun and holster were resting on top of the cabinet, and a newscaster was talking about the latest sanitation strike. A cigarette was in an ashtray on an end table alongside the easy chair. There were lipstick stains on its white filter tip. In the kitchen, Kling heard Ingersoll closing the refrigerator. He came into the room a moment later, glanced at a closed door at the far end, tilted the beer bottle to his lips, and drank. Briefly, he wiped the back of his hand across his mouth, and then said, "Something new on the case?"

"I think so, Mike."

"Not another burglary?"

"No, no."

"What then?"

"A positive identification," Kling said.

"Yeah? Great, great."

"That depends on where you're sitting, Mike."

"How do you mean?"

"Mrs. Ungerman called the squadroom earlier tonight. I was out, but I spoke to her just a little while ago." Kling paused. "She told me she knew who the burglar was. She hadn't made the connection before because she'd only seen him in . . ."

"Don't say it, Bert."

"She'd only seen him in uniform. But the other day, in the squadroom . . ."

"Don't, Bert."

"It's true, isn't it?"

Ingersoll did not answer.

"Mike? Is it true?"

"True or not, we can talk it over," Ingersoll said, and moved toward the television set.

"Don't go for the gun, Mike," Kling warned, and pulled his own service revolver.

"You don't need that, Bert," Ingersoll said with an injured tone.

"Don't I? Over there, Mike. Against the wall."

"Hey, come on . . ."

"*Move* it!"

"All right, take it easy, will you?" Ingersoll said, and backed away toward the wall.

"What'd you do, Mike? Steal a set of skeleton keys from the squadroom?"

"No."

"Then how'd you get them?"

"I was on a numbers investigation last October. Remember when they brought a lot of us in on . . ."

"Yes, I remember."

"We put in wires all around town. I was working with the tech guys who planted the bugs. That's when I got hold of the keys."

"What else are you into, Mike? Are you just burglarizing apartments?"

"Nothing, I swear!"

"Or are you selling dope to school kids, too?"

"Come on, Bert, what do you think I am?"

"I think you're a cheap thief!"

"I needed money!"

"We all need money!"

"Yeah, so name me a cop in the precinct who isn't on the take. When the hell did you get so fucking pure?"

"I've never taken a nickel, Mike."

"How many meals have you had on the arm?"

"Are you trying to equate a free cup of coffee with a string of felonies? Jesus Christ!"

"I'm trying to tell you . . ."

"Yeah, *what*, Mike?"

The room went silent. Ingersoll shrugged and said, "Look, I wanted to keep you out of this. Why do you think I suggested the stakeout? I didn't want anybody to think you were connected. I was . . ."

"The stakeout was a smoke screen, Kling said flatly. "That's why you wanted the walkie-talkies, isn't it? So I'd think you were sitting in the dark where you were *supposed* to be, when instead you were ripping off an apartment down the block. And the glass kitten! *'Guess he's running out of live ones,'* isn't that what you said, Mike? Running out, my ass. You couldn't carry a live one last night because even a dummy like me would've tipped to a goddamn cat in your coat pocket."

"Bert, believe me . . ."

"Oh, *I* believe you, Mike. It's the lieutenant who might not. Especially when he hears Fred Lipton's story."

"I have no connection with Fred Lipton."

"No? Well, we'll find out about that in just a little while, won't we? Hawes is picking him up right this minute. It's my guess he's your fence. Yes or no, Mike?"

"I told you I don't know him."

"Then why were you so anxious to get us off his trail? What'd you do, give Rhonda Spear a description of every cop in the squadroom? We were beginning to think she was a goddamn mind reader!" Kling paused, and then said, "Get her out here, Mike. We might as well take her along with us."

"What? Who?"

"The broad in the other room. It *is* Rhonda Spear, isn't it?"

"No, there's nobody . . ."

"Is she the one you were telling me about? The nice girl you want to marry, Mike? The reason you were so anxious to catch the burglar?"

"Bert . . ."

"Well, we've caught him. So how about introducing me to the bride? Miss!" he shouted. "Come out here with your hands over your head!"

"Don't shoot," a woman's voice said from behind the closed door. The door opened. A beefy blonde wearing a blue robe over a long pink nightgown came into the living room, her hands up over her head, her lip trembling.

"What's your name, miss?" Kling asked.

"Which one?" she asked.

"What?"

"Stage or real?"

"Are you Rhonda Spear?"

"Yes."

"Get dressed, Miss Spear. You, too, Mike."

"Bert, for Christ's sake . . . give me a break, will you?"

"Why?" Kling asked.

The motion picture had been a bad choice for Teddy Carella. It was full of arty shots in which the actors spoke from behind vases, trees, lampshades, or elephants, seemingly determined to hide their lips from her so that she would not know what was happening. When they weren't speaking with their faces hidden or their backs turned, the actors made important plot points offscreen, their voices floating in over the picture of a rushing locomotive or a changing traffic light.

Teddy normally enjoyed films, except when she was submitted to the excesses of a sadistic *nouvelle vague* camera. Tonight was such a night. She sat beside Carella and watched the film in utter helplessness, unable to "hear" long stretches of it, grateful when it ended and they could leave the theater.

It had been almost balmy when they'd left the house and they had elected to walk the six blocks to the theater on Dover Plains Avenue. The walk home was a bit chillier, the temperature having dropped slightly, but it was still comfortable, and they moved without hurry beside old trees that spread their branches over the deserted Riverhead sidewalks. Carella, in fact, seemed to be dawdling. Teddy was anxious to ask him all sorts of questions about the movie as soon as they got home; he was breathing deeply of the night air and walking the way an old man does in the park on Sunday morning, when there are pigeons to imitate.

The attack came without warning.

The fist was thrown full into his face, as unexpected as an earthquake. He was reaching for his gun when he was struck from behind by a second assailant. A third man grabbed for Teddy's handbag, just as the first attacker threw his clenched fist into Carella's face again. The man behind him was wielding a sap. Carella's gun came clear of his topcoat just as the sap grazed him above and behind the ear. There was the sound of the gun's explosion, shockingly loud on the still suburban street, and then the sap caught him again, solidly this time, at the base of the skull, and he toppled to the sidewalk.

The embarrassment was almost worse than the pain. A half hour later, in the muster room of the 103rd Precinct, he explained to an incredulous desk sergeant that he was a police officer and that he and his wife had been mugged on the way home from the movies. The attackers had stolen his wife's handbag and wristwatch, as well as his own watch, his wallet, and, most shameful to admit, his service revolver.

The sergeant took down all the information, and promised to get in touch.

Carella felt like a horse's ass.

Something was wrong with the day.

Heady breezes blew in off the River Harb, brilliant sunshine touched avenue and street; May was just around the corner, and April seemed bent on jubilant collision.

But there was no further communication from the Deaf Man. The first mail had already been delivered, and there was no manila envelope addressed to Carella, no duplication of the football team. Had this been an oversight, or was it a deliberate act of omission with deep significance? The detectives of the 87th Squad pondered this with the concern of a proctological convention considering oral hygiene. The case had been turned over to the stalwarts of the 86th; let *their* mothers worry.

•••

The clock on the sidewalk outside the bank read twelve minutes past nine. Sitting on a bench in the small park around which ran Van Buren Circle, the Deaf Man checked his own watch, and then glanced up the street. In three minutes, if the armored truck followed its usual Friday morning routine, enough cash to cover the combined McCormick, Meredith, and Holt payrolls would be delivered to the bank. At eleven o'clock, the money would be withdrawn, despite the efforts of the toy police, who were already inside the bank. The Deaf Man had seen them arriving at a little past nine, three burly detectives and one lady cop, undoubtedly there to replace the tellers. He credited them with having enough intelligence to realize he might strike at some time other than the announced eleven o'clock, but then even a cretin might have surmised that. And besides, they were wrong. The bank *would* be robbed at eleven. Whatever else the Deaf Man was, he was scrupulously fair. When dealing with inferiors, there was no other way.

The armored truck was coming up the street.

It pulled to the curb outside the bank. The driver got out and walked swiftly to the rear of the truck, taking up position near the door, a rifle in his hands. The door on the curbside opened, and the second guard got out and followed his partner, pistol still holstered. From a key attached to his belt with a chain, he unlocked the rear door of the truck. Then he took the pistol from its holster, turned up the butt, and rapped sharply on the door, twice, the signal for the guard inside to unlock the door from within. The rear door of the truck opened. The guard with the rifle covered his companions as they transferred the two sacks of cash from the truck to the pavement. The guard inside the truck climbed down, pistol in hand,

and picked up one of the sacks. The second guard picked up the other sack. As they walked toward the revolving doors, the guard with the rifle covered the sidewalk. It was all very routine, and all very efficient.

As they disappeared inside the bank, the Deaf Man nodded, smiled, and walked swiftly to a pay phone on the corner. He dialed his own number, and the phone on the other end was lifted on the second ring.

"Hello?" a voice said.

"Kerry?"

"Yes?"

"This is Mr. Taubman."

"Yes, Mr. Taubman."

"The money is here. You and the others may come for it at once."

"Thank you, Mr. Taubman."

There was a click on the line. Still smiling, the Deaf Man replaced the receiver on the hook and went back to his command post on the park bench.

Inside the bank, Detective Schmitt of the 86th was briefing Mr. Alton yet another time. The clock on the wall opposite the tellers' cages read 9:21.

"There's nothing to worry about," Schmitt said. "I've got experienced men at windows number one and two, and an experienced policewoman at the car teller's window. I'll be covering window number three myself."

"Yes, thank you," Alton said. He hesitated, and glanced nervously around the bank. "What do I do meanwhile?"

"Just go about your business as usual," Schmitt said. "Try to relax. There's no sense upsetting your customers. Everything's under control. Believe me, Mr.

Alton, with the four of us here, nobody's going to rob this bank."

Schmitt didn't realize it, but he was right.

At 9:37 A.M. Kerry Donovan, his head shaved bald and gleaming in the sun, a new but nonetheless rather respectable mustache under his nose, entered the bank carrying a large black rectangular case. He asked the guard where the manager's office was, and the guard asked whether he had an appointment. Donovan said yes, he had called last week to make an appointment with Mr. Alton. The guard asked Donovan his name, and he replied, "Mr. Dunmore. Karl Dunmore."

"One second, Mr. Dunmore," the guard said, and signaled to one of the bank clerks, an attractive young girl in her twenties, who immediately came over to him.

"Mr. Karl Dunmore to see Mr. Alton," the guard said.

"Just a moment, please," the girl said, and walked to the rear of the bank and into Alton's office. She came out not a moment later, walked back to where the guard and Donovan were engaged in polite conversation about the beautiful weather, and asked Donovan if he would come with her, please. Donovan followed her up the length of the bank, passing the Deaf Man, who stood at one of the islands making out a deposit slip. She opened the door to Alton's office, ushered him in, and closed the door behind him.

The Deaf Man thought it a pity that Kerry Donovan did not know the bank was full of policemen.

"Mr. Dunmore," Alton said, and extended his hand. "Nice to see you."

"Good of you to make time for me," Donovan said.

"What have you brought me?"

"Well, as we discussed on the phone, I thought we might make more progress once you'd actually seen the plans and scale model of our project. I know we're asking for an unusually large amount of development money, but I'm hoping you'll agree our expectations for profit are realistic. May I use your desk top?" Donovan asked, and quickly realized that the model was too big for Alton's cluttered desk. "Or perhaps the floor would be better," be said, improvising. "We can spread the plans out that way, get a better look at them."

"Yes, certainly," Alton said. "As you wish."

Donovan opened the black case and carefully removed from it a scale model of a forty-unit housing development, complete with winding roads, miniature trees, lampposts, and fire hydrants. He put this on the floor in front of the desk, and then reached into the case for a rolled sheaf of architectural drawings. He removed the rubber band from the roll, and spread the plans on the floor.

"I wonder if I could have something to hold these down?" he said.

"Will this do?" Alton asked.

"Yes, thank you," Donovan said, and accepted the offered cut-glass paperweight. "Just to hold down this one end of it."

"Yes," Alton said.

"If you'll come around here, Mr. Alton, I think you'll be able to . . ."

"Where's the proposed location?" Alton said, coming around the desk.

"I explained that in my initial . . ."

"Yes, but we deal with so many . . ."

"It's on Sands Spit, sir."

"Have you sought development money out there?"

"No, sir. Our offices are here in Isola. We thought it preferable to deal with a local bank."

"I see."

"This top drawing is a schematic of the entire development. If you compare it with the model . . ."

Alton was standing just to Donovan's left now, looking down at the model. Donovan rose, drew a pistol from his coat pocket, and pointed it at Alton's head.

"Don't make a sound," he said. "This is a holdup. Do exactly what I tell you to do, or I'll kill you."

Alton, his lip trembling, stared at the muzzle of the gun. The Deaf Man had deliberately armed Donovan with a Colt .45, the meanest-looking handgun he could think of.

"Do you understand?" Donovan asked.

"Yes. Yes, I do."

"Good. We're going into the vault now," Donovan said, and stopped, and quickly snapped the case shut. "If we meet anyone on the way, you're to tell them I'm here to inspect the alarm. If there's anyone in the vault, you will ask that person to leave us alone. Clear?"

"Yes."

"No signals to anyone, no attempts to indicate that anything out of the ordinary is happening. I promise you, Mr. Alton, a felony conviction will send me to jail for life, and I have no qualms about shooting you dead. I'm going to put this gun back in my pocket now, but it'll be pointed right at you, Mr. Alton, and I'll fire through the pocket if you so much as raise an eyebrow to anyone. Are you ready?"

"Yes, I'm ready."

"Let's go then."

• • •

From where he stood at the island in the center of the bank, the Deaf Man saw Donovan and Alton coming out of the office and heading for the vault. Donovan was smiling and chatting amiably, the black case in his left hand, his right hand in the pocket of his coat. Both men went into the vault, and the Deaf Man headed swiftly toward the revolving doors at the front of the bank. According to the outlined plan, he was supposed to initiate the second phase of the plan only *after* Donovan was safely out of the vault and back in the manager's office. Instead, he walked out of the bank now, his appearance on the sidewalk being the signal to the two automobiles parked on the other side of the small park. He saw Rudy Manello pulling the first car away from the curb. Angela Gould's car followed immediately behind it. In less than a minute Rudy had driven around the curving street and turned into the driveway on the right-hand side of the bank, Angela following in the second automobile. When Angela's car was directly abreast of the driveway, she cut the engine, and pretended helpless female indignation at things mechanical. An instant later John Preiss stepped out of the first car and swung a sledge hammer at the car teller's window.

An instant after that, both he and Rudy were shot dead by the policewoman behind the shattered window. Kerry Donovan, still in the bank vault stuffing banded stacks of bills into the black case, heard the shots and realized at once that something had gone wrong. He dropped the bills in his hand, rushed out of the vault, saw that the woman in the car teller's window was armed, and recognized in panic that he could not make his escape as planned. He was running for the revolving doors at the front of the bank when he was felled by bullets from the guns of the three separate detectives manning the interior tellers' cages.

Outside the bank Angela Gould heard all the shooting and immediately started the car. In her panic she would not have stopped to pick up the Deaf Man even if he'd been waiting on the sidewalk where he was supposed to be. But by that time he was in a taxicab half a mile away, heading for a rendezvous with the second team.

Something was still wrong with the day, only more so.

When Albert Schmitt of the 86th called Carella to report that the attempted robbery had been foiled, Carella was somewhat taken aback.

"What do you mean?" he asked, and looked up at the wall clock. "It's only ten-thirty."

"That's right," Schmitt said. "They hit early."

"When?"

"Almost an hour ago. They came in about twenty to ten. It was all over by ten."

"Who? How many?"

"One guy inside, two outside. I don't know what the plan was, but how they ever expected to get away with it is beyond me. Especially after all the warning beforehand. I don't get it, Carella, I really don't."

"Who were the men involved in the attempt?" Carella asked.

"Identification we found on the bodies . . ."

"They're all dead?"

"All three of them. Rudy Manello, John Preiss, and Kerry Donovan. Names mean anything to you?"

"Nothing at all. Any of them wearing a hearing aid?"

"A what?"

"A hearing aid."

"No."

"Any of them tall and blond?"

"No."

"Then he got away."

"Who did?"

"The guy who masterminded it."

"Some mastermind," Schmitt said. "My six-year-old kid could've planned a better caper. It's like nothing ever happened, Carella. The glazier already had the window fixed before I left. I pulled my people out because even the guys from the security office were leaving. Anyway, we can forget about it now. It's all over and done with."

"Well, good," Carella said, "good," and hung up feeling mildly disappointed. The squadroom was unusually silent, the windows open to the sounds of light morning traffic. Carella sat at his desk and sipped coffee from a cardboard container. This was not like the Deaf Man. If Carella had figured him correctly (and he probably hadn't), the "delicate symbiosis" of which he had spoken was composed of several interlocking elements.

Not the least of these was the Deaf Man himself. It now seemed apparent that he worked with different pickup gangs on each job, rather like a jazz soloist recruiting sidemen in the various cities on his tour. In the past any apprehended gang members did not know the true identity of their leader; he had presented himself once as L. Sordo and again as Mort Orecchio, the former name meaning "the deaf one" in Spanish, the latter meaning "dead ear" in Italian. The hearing aid itself may have been a phony, even though he always took pains to announce that he was hard of hearing. But whatever he was or whoever he was, the crimes he conceived were always grand in scale and involved large sums of money.

Nor was conceiving crimes and executing them quite enough for the Deaf Man. The second symbiotic element consisted of telling the police what he was going to do long before he did it. At first Carella had supposed this to be evidence of a monumental ego, but he had come to learn that the Deaf Man used the police as a sort of *second* pickup gang, larger than the nucleus group, but equally essential to the successful commission of the crime. That he had been thwarted on two previous occasions was entirely due to chance. He was smarter than the police, and he used the police, and he let the police know they were being used, and that was where the third element locked into place.

Knowing they were being used, but not *how*; knowing he was telling them a great deal about the crime, but not *enough*; knowing he would do what he predicted, but not *exactly*, the police generally reacted like country bumpkins on a hick police force. Their behavior in turn strengthened the Deaf Man's premise that they were singularly inept. Given their now-demonstrated ineffectiveness, he became more and more outrageous, more and more daring. And the bolder *he* became, the more *they* tripped over their own flat feet. It was, indeed, a delicate symbiosis.

But the deception this time seemed unworthy of someone of his caliber. The cheapest thief in the precinct could just as easily have announced that he would rob a bank at eleven and then rob it at nine-thirty. Big deal. A lie of such petty dimensions hardly required duplication. Yet the Deaf Man had thought it necessary to tell them all about it twice. So apparently he himself was convinced that he was about to pull off the biggest caper in the history of criminal endeavor, gigantic enough to be announced not only once, but then once again—like 50 DANCING GIRLS 50.

Carella picked up the container and sipped at his coffee. It was getting cold. He swallowed the remainder of it in a single gulp and then almost choked on the startling suddenness of an exceptionally brilliant thought: the Deaf Man had *not* said everything twice. True enough, he had said almost everything twice, but there had been only *one* photostat pinpointing the time of the holdup. Carella shoved back his chair and reached for his jacket. He had brought another gun to work with him this morning, the first revolver he'd owned, back when he was a patrolman. He eased it out of the holster now, the grip unfamiliar to him, and hoped he would not have to use it, hoped somehow he was wrong. But it was a quarter to eleven on the face of the squadroom clock, and Carella now thought he knew why there'd been any duplication at all, and it did not have a damn thing to do with his twins or the Deaf Man's ego.

Oddly, it had only to do with playing the crime game fair.

He came through the revolving doors at ten minutes to eleven, walked directly to the bank guard, and opened his wallet.

"Detective Carella," he said, "87th Squad. I'd like to see Mr. Alton, please."

The bank guard studied the detective's shield pinned to a leather tab opposite an identification card. He nodded, and then said, "Right this way, sir," and led him through the bank to a door at the far end, adjacent to the vault. Discreetly, he knocked.

"Yes?" a voice said.

"It's me, Mr. Alton. Corrigan."

"Come in," Alton said.

The bank guard entered the office, and came out again not a moment later. "Go right in, Mr. Carella," he said.

Alton was sitting behind his desk, but he rose and extended his hand at once. "How do you do?" he said.

"How do you do, sir? I'm Detective Carella of the 87th Squad." He showed his shield and I.D. card again, and then smiled. "How do you feel after all that excitement?" he asked, and pulled a chair up to the desk, and sat.

"Much better now," Alton said. "What can I do for you, Detective Carella?"

"Well, sir, I won't be more than a few minutes. We're the squad that caught the original squeal and later turned it over to the 86th. My lieutenant asked me to stop by and complete this check list, if that's okay with you."

"What sort of check list?" Alton asked.

"Well, sir, I hate to bother you with interdepartmental problems, but that's exactly what this is, and I hope you'll bear with me. You see, because the case was turned over to another squad, that doesn't mean it isn't still officially ours. The final disposition of it, I mean."

"I'm not sure I understand," Alton said.

"We're responsible for it, sir. It's as simple as that."

"I see," Alton said, but he still looked puzzled.

"These questions are just to make sure that the 86th handled things properly. I'll be honest with you, Mr. Alton, it's our insurance in case there's any static later on. From the brass upstairs, I mean."

"I see," Alton said, finally comprehending. "What are the questions?"

"Just a few, sir," he said, and took a sheet of paper from his pocket, unfolded it, and put it on the desk. There were several typewritten questions on the sheet. He took out a ballpoint pen, glanced at the first question, and said, "How many police officers were inside the bank at the time of the attempted robbery?"

"Four," Alton said.

"Would you know their names?"

"The man in charge was Detective Schmitt. I don't know the names of the others."

"I can get that from the 86th," he said, and wrote "Schmitt" on the typewritten sheet, and then went on to the next question. "Were you treated courteously by the police at all times?"

"Oh yes, most definitely," Alton said.

He wrote the word "Yes" alongside the question, and then said, "Did any of the police officers have access to cash while they were inside the bank?"

"Yes. The ones at the tellers' windows."

"Has this cash been tallied since the police officers left the bank?"

"No, Mr. Carella, it has not."

"When will a tally be made?"

"This afternoon."

"Would you please give me a call after the tally is made, sir? The number is Frederick 7-8025."

"Yes, I'll do that."

"Just so I'll know it's all there," he said, and smiled.

"Yes," Alton said.

"Just a few more questions. Did any of the police officers enter the vault at any time while they were inside the bank?"

"No."

"Sir, can you tell me how much cash was actually delivered to the bank this morning?"

"Five hundred thousand, three hundred dollars."

"Was it counted after the holdup, sir?"

"It was."

"By whom?"

"My assistant manager. Mr. Warshaw."

"Was it all there?"

"Every penny."

"Then the perpetrators were entirely unsuccessful."

"Entirely."

"Good. I'd like to get Mr. Warshaw's signature later, stating that he counted the money after the attempted holdup and after the police officers had left the bank . . ."

"Well, they were still *in* the bank while he was counting."

"But not in the vault?"

"No."

"That's just as good, Mr. Alton. I only need verification, that's all. Could we go into the vault now?"

"The vault? What for?"

"To satisfy my lieutenant's request."

"What *is* your lieutenant's request, Detective Carella?"

"He wants me to make sure the cash is all there."

"I've just told you it's all there."

"He wants me to ascertain the fact, sir."

"How?"

"By counting it."

"That's absurd," Alton said, and looked at his watch. "We'll be sending the cash out to the tellers in just a little while. An accurate count would take you . . ."

"I'll be very quick about it, Mr. Alton. Would it be all right if we went into the vault now? So I can get started?"

"No, I don't think so," Alton said.

"Why not, sir?"

"I've just told you. I don't mind cooperating with a departmental request, but not if it's going to further upset the bank's routine. I've had enough confusion here today, and I don't need . . ."

"Sir, this is more than just a departmental request. In order to close out the investigation and satisfy my lieutenant's . . ."

"Perhaps I'd best discuss this with your lieutenant then," Alton said, and reached for the telephone. "What did you say your number was?"

"Don't touch that phone, Mr. Alton."

The man was holding a revolver in his fist, and pointing it directly at Alton's head. For a moment Alton had a terrible feeling of *déja vu.* He thought, No, this cannot possibly be happening twice in the same day, and then he heard the man saying, "Now listen to me very carefully, Mr. Alton. We are going into the vault and you are going to tell anyone we meet on the way or in the vault itself that I am Detective Carella of the 87th Squad and that we are taking the cash to your office for a count according to police regulations. If you say anything to the contrary, I'll put a hole in your fucking head. Have you got that, Mr. Alton?"

Alton sighed and said, "Yes, I've got it."

From where he stood at the island counter, the Deaf Man saw Harold and Alton leaving the manager's office. Harold's right hand was in the pocket of his coat, undoubtedly around the butt of his pistol. He watched as they entered the vault. On the withdrawal slip before him, he wrote the date, and the number of his account, and then he filled in the amount as *Five hundred thousand and no/100*, and in the space provided wrote the amount in numerals, *$500,000*, and then signed the slip *D. R. Taubman.*

Alton was coming out of the vault already, carrying a sack of cash. Harold was directly behind him, carrying the second sack, his right hand still in his coat pocket. Together, they went into Alton's office. The door closed behind them, and the Deaf Man started for the front of the bank.

He was feeling quite proud of himself. Folklore maintained that lightning never struck twice, especially within the space of less than an hour and a half. Yet Harold already had all that sweet cash in his possession, and in just several minutes more (as soon as the Deaf Man stepped outside the bank) Danny and Roger would drive up to the car teller's window, Florence would park her car across the driveway, and the robbery would happen all over again. The only difference was that this time it would work. It would work because it had already failed, and nobody expects failure to be an essential *part* of any plan. Having foiled a daring robbery attempt, everyone was now content to sit back and bask in the glory of the achievement. When that teller's window was smashed in just a very few minutes, and the alarm sounded at the 86th Precinct and the Security Office, the Deaf Man would not be surprised if everyone considered it an error. He was willing to bet that the phone in Mr. Alton's office would ring immediately, asking if this was legit or if there was something malfunctioning. In any case, Harold would be out of the office the moment he heard the glass smashing, and they would all be on their way before the police responded. It was almost too simple. And yet it was delicious.

He reached the revolving doors and started through them.

A man was pushing his way through from the street side.

It had been a long time since the Deaf Man had seen Carella. But when you've once fired a shotgun at a man and he later returns the compliment with a .38 Detective's Special, you're not too terribly likely to forget his face. The Deaf Man knew at once that the man shoving his way into the bank was Detective Steve Carella, whom his cohorts had clobbered and robbed of identification the night before. In that split second of recognition, the Deaf Man found himself *outside* the bank, while Carella moved *inside* and walked directly to the guard.

Carella had not seen him.

But the Deaf Man's appearance on the sidewalk was the signal for Roger and Danny to start their car and head for the teller's window, which they did now with frightening alacrity. Similarly, it was the signal for Florence to move *her* car across the mouth of the bank's driveway, and the Deaf Man was dismayed to see that she had learned her job only too well, and was proceeding to perform it with all possible haste. Carella was talking to the bank guard, who looked extremely puzzled, as well he might when presented with two detectives in the space of fifteen minutes, each of whom claimed to be the same person. The Deaf Man figured the jig was up. He did what any sensible master criminal would have done in the same situation. He got the hell out of there, fast.

A lot of things happened in the next few minutes.

Following the guard to the manager's office, Carella heard glass shattering on his right. He turned and saw a man smashing the car teller's window with a sledge hammer. He did what any sensible crack detective would have done in the same situation. He drew his revolver and fired at the man, and then ran to the counter and fired across it at a second man, sitting in the driver's seat of a car outside the window. In that instant a third man came running out of the manager's office carrying two sacks of cash. The bank guard, thinking he had somehow lived through all of this before, in the not-too-distant past, nonetheless drew his own pistol and began firing at the man with the cash, whom he had previously met as Detective Carella; it was all very confusing. He hit the vault door, he hit the door to Mr. Alton's office, and he also hit Mr. Warshaw, the assistant manager, in the right arm. But he did not hit the man carrying the sacks of cash. The man dropped one sack, pulled a pistol from his coat pocket, and began spraying the center aisle with bullets. He leaped the counter, and was heading for the broken teller's window when Carella shot him in the leg. He whirled and, dragging himself toward the window, fired at Carella, shoved the frightened car teller out of his way, and attempted to climb through the broken glass to where one of his colleagues lay dead at the wheel of the car. Carella felled him with his second shot, and then leaped the counter himself and rushed to the broken window. The man who had smashed it with the sledge hammer was badly wounded and trying to crawl up the driveway to where a car engine suddenly started. Carella leaned out and fired at the car as it pulled away, tires screeching. One of the lady tellers screamed. A uniformed policeman rushed into the bank and starting firing at Carella, who yelled, "I'm a cop!" And then the bank was swarming with policemen from the 86th and private security officers, all of them answering the alarm for the second time that day. Two blocks away from the bank, the lady driving the getaway car ran a traffic light and was stopped by a patrolman. She tried to shoot him with a .22 caliber revolver she pulled from her purse, so the patrolman hit her with his nightstick and clapped her into handcuffs.

Her name was Florence Barrows.

Florence had once told the Deaf Man that she'd never met a man she could trust and didn't expect anyone to trust her, either.

She told the detectives everything she knew.

"His name is Taubman," she said, "and we had our meetings in a room at the Hotel Remington. Room 604. I'd never met him before he contacted me for the caper, and I don't know anything else about him."

This time, they had him.

They didn't expect to find anybody at the Hotel Remington, and they didn't. But now, at least, they had a name for him. They began going through all the city directories, encouraged by the scarcity of Taubmans, determined to track down each and every one of them until they got their man—even if it took forever.

It did not take nearly that long.

Detective Schmitt of the 86th Squad called while they were still going through the directories and compiling a list of Taubmans.

"Hey, how *about* that?" he said to Carella. "Son of a bitch really *did* try to bring it off at eleven, huh?"

"He sure did," Carella said.

"I understand he got away, though," Schmitt said.

"Yeah, but we've got a lead."

"Oh? What've you got?"

"His name."

"Great. Has he got a record?"

"We're checking that with the I.S. right this minute."

"Good, good. Is it a common name?"

"Only eleven of them in the Isola directory. Five in Calm's Point. We're checking the others now."

"What's the name?" Schmitt asked.

"Taubman."

"Yeah?"

"Yeah," Carella said. There had been a curious lilt to Schmitt's voice just then, a mixture of incredulity and mirth. "Why?" Carella, asked at once.

"Didn't you say the guy was deaf?"

"Yes, I did. What . . . ?"

"Because, you know . . . I *guess* you know . . . or maybe you don't."

"What?"

"It's German. Taubman."

"So?"

"It means the deaf man. *'Der taube mann.'* That means 'the deaf man' in German."

"I see," Carella said.

"Yeah," Schmitt said.

"Thank you," Carella said.

"Don't mention it," Schmitt said, and hung up.

Carella put the phone back onto its cradle and decided to become a fireman.